"Max!" His name was ripped from her

There was no answer. Kate ran back to the living area and searched for a note. Max wasn't there. He would have left a note. Surely after last night he'd leave a note. Surely he would.

Max wasn't the kind of man to walk away without a goodbye. It wasn't his style. There must be some explanation.

But as Kate tore through the suite, she could find no trace of Max.

Max was gone.

Dear Reader,

Just before I graduated from college, an Alpha Gam sorority sister gave each of the seniors a quote in beautiful calligraphy expressing a sentiment she felt represented us. Mine was a quote from the American writer, Langston Hughes: "Hold fast to dreams, for if dreams die, life is a broken-winged bird that cannot fly."

How appropriate that quote turned out to be. I believe in trying to make dreams come true, and so do my heroines—and it's while they're pursuing their dreams that they meet their true love. (I met my true love in high school government class. I was not pursuing a dream at the time.)

In *Undercover Lover,* Kate's family was wise enough to let her pursue her dream even though it took her away from them. Being able to live her own life was so important to her that during the book she's trying to make it possible for her brother to have his dream. Max has a dream as well, and it's while he's chasing his dream that he meets Kate.

I hope you're following your dreams. I found a wonderful piece of advice in last Sunday's comics, an odd place to find profound philosophies, but here it is: "Whether you succeed or not, you shouldn't think of yourself as a failure because in order to fail, you have to be one of the ones who tried."

Sweet dreams!

Heather Allison

Undercover
Lover
Heather Allison

Harlequin Books

TORONTO • NEW YORK • LONDON
AMSTERDAM • PARIS • SYDNEY • HAMBURG
STOCKHOLM • ATHENS • TOKYO • MILAN
MADRID • WARSAW • BUDAPEST • AUCKLAND

To my grandmother, Mildred Hull.

ISBN 0-373-03386-9

UNDERCOVER LOVER

First North American Publication 1995.

Copyright © 1995 by Heather W. MacAllister.

PROLOGUE

A *GLOBAL CELEBRITY* EXCLUSIVE! We were there!

Actress Fiona Ferguson's wedding! Stars galore! Photos inside!

At Miss Ferguson's express invitation, *Global Celebrity* photographers captured her nuptials to wealthy Chicago businessman Winthrop Perrine.

The two reportedly met just six weeks ago at a Hollywood charity gala underwritten by the Xavier Group, of which Perrine is CEO.

Just after the ceremony, Fiona, flashing a five-carat diamond engagement ring, (close-up on page two) gazed adoringly at her husband. "At last I've found my true love."

The seventy-three-year-old Perrine refused to comment on the four-decade difference in their ages, though when asked about his wife's reputation for falling in love with her leading men, he declared, "I'm her leading man now."

CHAPTER ONE

KATE Brandon wanted to shoot Fiona Ferguson. And if the woman would move a few inches to the left, Kate could get a clear shot at her.

Soft laughter drifted on the late-afternoon breeze as Kate's target lounged behind an open car door.

"Come on, walk back into the house, Fiona," Kate muttered under her breath. The three-hundred-millimeter telephoto lens scraped the rose-tinted rock of the security wall as she steadied her camera.

If Fiona Ferguson would take off the sunglasses and hat, Kate was assured of paying her hotel bill. If Fiona stepped from behind the limousine door, it was worth three months' rent and a full refrigerator.

But if a sunglasses-less, hatless Fiona were photographed with Damian Carney—who Kate suspected was just inside the doorway of the rented villa on the island of Capri—Kate would be sitting pretty for the next year.

And if Fiona kissed him...

Steady. Kate couldn't think about the possibilities without her hands shaking. Of course, that might be due to hunger. She'd been staking out the villa all day, as she had been for the past week. Her sandwich was long gone, and usually by now, so was Kate, but there had been unaccustomed activity at the villa today.

Fiona and Damian might be leaving and returning to the set of the movie they were filming together.

So far, they'd been discreet. After all, Fiona was newly married and Damian's wife had publicly stated that one more affair and he'd be involved in a very expensive divorce. Only whispers of the two stars' involvement had wafted back to Kate's contacts at *World Eye*. But Kate had excellent hearing—especially when it concerned Fiona Ferguson.

The fiery Irish actress had left her new husband behind in Chicago—her rich, older, Midwestern conservative husband. The same husband who had been talked into backing Fiona's latest movie.

Kate hadn't been able to get any good photos of the wedding. It had been an alluring mix of Hollywood glitterati and business-world establishment. Security was experienced, tight and professional. Not that Kate wasn't professional, but Fiona had wisely sold exclusive rights to her wedding.

Unfortunately, she'd sold them to *Global Celebrity*, one of Kate's competitors.

Win some, lose some. Kate mentally shrugged at the memory, though it still stung.

No sooner had the unlikely pair returned from their honeymoon when Fiona announced that she and her groom were forming a production company. To no one's surprise, the first project was a movie starring Fiona Ferguson.

Fiona's legendary temper and unpredictability had scared off most directors and producers. This was to be her second chance. A second chance she should be protecting instead of jeopardizing her marriage—and her movie—by having a fling with her leading man.

Sure he was handsome, Kate supposed, but was he *really* worth the risk?

Was any man?

Luckily for her, Fiona seemed to think so. Kate hunched her shoulders and stretched her arms, one at a time, keeping her camera ready. What was that woman doing? Why didn't she just get in the car and drive away so Kate could climb down off this stepladder and go back to her grungy motel? It crossed her mind that Fiona might suspect photographers were hiding among the citrus trees bordering the villa's gardens and enjoyed toying with them. Only someone with an ego the size of Fiona's would tempt fate that way.

Gingerly, Kate flexed first one leg, then the other and wiped her eyes on her bare arm. The sun slid lower in the sky. In minutes, the rays would pierce her leafy cover and shine into her lens making any usable shots impossible.

A car passed on the narrow, cliffside road behind her and Kate's subconscious noted it. The car wasn't moving as fast as normal traffic, not that this road, winding in the steep cliffs, had much traffic at all. That probably meant another photographer was searching for a spot to spy on the villa. Her own car was pulled well off the road, but not hidden. Any of the paparazzi who covered glittering Capri could figure out she was here. And why.

Kate sighed. She'd followed Fiona on a hunch, and she couldn't expect to be the only photographer with hunches. But Fiona Ferguson was *her* speciality. Early in both their careers, Kate had concentrated on photographing Fiona for various celebrity pictorials because of the redhead's innate star quality. The woman was going somewhere and Kate hoped to go right along with her. And, practical Kate also found Fiona's vivid red hair easier to pick out in a crowd than other less flamboyant personalities.

They'd even become friends for a while—until Kate's younger brother, Jonathan, had come to visit. Fiona charmed him, then dumped him with a breathtaking callousness that Jonathan couldn't accept and Kate couldn't forgive.

A flash caught Kate's eyes and she scanned the trees to her left. Was that the reflection of the sun on another camera?

Or just the fabulous diamond bracelet Fiona wore everywhere?

Searching the length of the stone security wall, Kate looked for another black lens, looked for another pair of hands. She listened for the telltale click of a shutter and the whir of the auto-advance, and heard nothing but the guard dogs barking in the distance.

The flash must have come from the diamonds. While she waited for a recognizable shot, Kate zoomed in on the actress's wrist, propped on the car door.

Gaudy thing, Kate thought as she popped off a couple of useless shots. Useless, because that bracelet, a wedding gift from Fiona's adoring husband, had been well photographed.

However, Kate brightened, it would prove the identity of the woman in the driveway, should she need to. Gad, look at that display of diamonds—and before five o'clock, too.

The whir of her own camera automatically advancing to the next frame sounded unnaturally loud.

For a moment, Kate imagined Fiona might have heard, because she swiveled her head to search the perimeter of the villa's terraced gardens. Kate was yards away, but visible, if one knew where to look and one had excellent eyesight.

Fiona was staring straight at her...or it seemed that way. With those sunglasses, Kate couldn't really be certain.

Maybe Fiona'd take them off...Kate's finger moved over the shutter release. Maybe Damian was coming out.

Kate risked lifting her eyes from the viewfinder to observe the whole area. The movement caused the front legs of the stepladder to sink an inch farther into the moist decomposing layer of vegetation at the base of the wall.

Propping her elbows against the wall, Kate settled in. She'd already had to move the ladder twice. At least it was cooler here than the view she'd found overlooking the swimming pool. That hadn't panned out, though Kate wasn't surprised. The fair-skinned Fiona shunned the sun.

What a waste to be here on one of the most famous resort islands in the world and not swim in the deep blue waters. Kate could stand a quick dunk. Maybe explore the famous caves. She'd never seen the Blue Grotto—

Suitcases! At the top of the steps, a chauffeur appeared and carried two matched bags to the car. More followed.

Kate shot four more frames. Okay, now she was getting something. It meant that as soon as the limo was loaded and Fiona and Damian were driven away, Kate would follow them to the dock—assuming they were on their way back to Sorrento. But they had to be; didn't they have a movie to film?

Fiona, with another scan of the garden area, ducked into the car.

Kate sighed, but kept her camera poised. A montage wasn't as valuable as the two stars in the same frame, but it would be worth something to her editor.

The chauffeur appeared with more luggage. A different set.

Okay. That would be Damian's. Kate flexed her shoulders and peered through the viewfinder, snapping a picture of the open trunk and all the luggage. She'd get what pictures she could here and then race them to the marina. Rather than taking the ferry, they were probably leaving by private boat. She might get the two of them together there.

The dogs were still barking, louder now. Something had set them off. Another photographer? Reporters?

Rats, the beasts were coming her way.

At least she was on the other side of an eight-foot-high security wall.

The chauffeur closed the trunk and walked around to the passenger side of the car and stood by the door, his back to Kate. She pointed her lens and focused moments before Damian Carney ran lightly down the steps.

Kate got off four, maybe five photos of the handsome blond actor, the dogs' barking drowning out the sound of her camera motor.

Cradling her camera, Kate hopped off the stepladder and snapped on a lens cap, grabbed for the ladder and ran toward her car.

She emerged from the trees and froze.

There was her car, all right, but galloping toward it were two Doberman pinschers. What were they doing *outside* the wall?

Kate judged the distance to her car and the rate of the Dobermans' approach and realized they'd all arrive at the same time. Great. She could either tumble down the cliffs, or scale the wall. Or try to reason with the snarling dogs.

She hadn't given Fiona enough credit, Kate thought as she raced toward the stone wall. She intended to climb the stepladder and vault over the top of the wall. Technically, she'd be trespassing, but trespassing was better than being eaten.

Slinging her camera and lenses so they hung down her back, Kate scrambled up the ladder and grabbed the top of the wall.

"Hey! Over here!" A man's voice sounded over the dogs' yapping.

Was he shouting at her or the dogs? Kate ignored him, hoping he was the properly horrified owner of the runaway beasts. Hoping that Fiona hadn't sent the dogs to attack her.

"I've got a car!"

Bully for him. Kate jumped and swung her leg over the top of the wall.

"Don't climb over. You'll be trapped inside!"

Through the trees, Kate saw a black car pulled over to the side of the road. A dark-haired man stood beside the open door and gestured urgently. "Get in!"

Right, as if she'd run and hop into the car of a total stranger. She'd rather face the Dobermans.

Waving, Kate swung her other leg over and prepared for an eight-foot drop.

"What're you doing? Are you *nuts*?"

He glanced from her to the approaching dogs then back to her, his face a mixture of disbelief and exasperation.

Just as Kate held her camera and scooted off her perch, she registered the fact that the man had spoken in unaccented English.

She landed and fell forward on her knees, staying crouched and listening. Within moments, a car door slammed and the motor gunned. Seconds after that, the dogs arrived at a howl. She could hear them jumping up and down, barking all the while.

The front of the villa was deserted, but Kate expected the staff to come running.

Now, she was trespassing. Now, she could be arrested.

Yes, she'd underestimated Fiona. Damian must have taught her this trick.

Kate stood and brushed off her knees. She'd never expected the dogs *outside* the wall. Either someone had spotted Kate's car, or this was a cautionary measure.

It was certainly effective. By the time Kate had made her way back to her car, Fiona and Damian would be across the bay in Sorrento.

And the two of them didn't appear together in one frame of Kate's film.

Where now? The front gate, she supposed, even though her car was in the opposite direction. She'd have to hike around. The stupid dogs were still barking and carrying on.

Setting off at a brisk walk across the terraces, she scanned the villa for signs of life. *Somebody* had to come for the dogs.

On cue, a whistle pierced the endless yapping.

Doomed. She was doomed.

Halfheartedly, Kate picked up speed.

But, signore, I'd only stopped my car to answer a call of nature when I was set upon by these vicious animals. The call of nature excuse had worked before, but only with men. Besides, there was the camera to explain.

Officer, I'm so glad to see you! The view of the marina is perfect from here and I was only taking pictures when I was attacked by dogs. I was so frightened . . . Hmm. Maybe not.

Look, we both know I can press charges against you for allowing your dogs to run loose outside the grounds. How about you forget the trespassing and I won't mention that your puppies escaped?

The iron grille of the front gate loomed ahead. Maybe she'd get lucky and wouldn't have to talk her way out of anything. There was only an occasional distant yip out of the dogs and the inhabitants of the villa were not in evidence.

She might make it.

Cheering up, Kate jogged the last few feet and pushed against the gate.

It was locked. Of course.

She gripped the bars and rested her head against them, catching her breath.

Okay. It could be worse. If she had to, she could wait until dark, then drag the pool furniture over and use it to scale the wall.

By then, she had no doubt that her rental car would be towed away and traced to her.

By then, the dogs would be roaming the grounds.

Kate rattled the gate in frustration. The road was right *there*. Freedom was inches away.

All right. She was going to climb the wall. There was bound to be a section with footholds or even a door. Kate took two steps away before becoming aware of another sound.

In the distance, but growing closer, was the two-toned whine of a police siren.

And the frenzied yapping of dogs.

Oh, great. Eaten *and* arrested.

Kate took a deep breath. If the police didn't hurry up, there wouldn't be anything left of her to arrest. She could tell the dogs were now back inside the walls and hot on the trail of an intruder—*her* trail.

A sirenless black car, probably the local police chief thrilled to have an excuse to hobnob with movie stars, pulled off the road and Kate ran back to the gate.

"Hurry up, the dogs are coming!" she yelled as the car door opened. At the same moment, she realized that the black car was the same one she'd seen before.

"I know. I can hear 'em." The man who'd so urgently beckoned to her earlier, now casually emerged from the car, closed the door and leaned against it, arms crossed.

They stared at each other.

His hair was a little too long, his jeans were a little too worn and his smile was a little too smug.

He was Kate's only hope. "Can you open this gate?"

"No."

She could hardly hear him, what with the sirens and the dogs. "Are you just going to stand there?"

"That's up to you."

Kate glanced behind her. Boy, those dogs could run fast. "I'm going to be mincemeat in a minute!"

He didn't move.

"Ram the gate with your car," she urged him. "I'll pay for damages."

"Rescue you, in other words," he said, his smile still in place.

"Whatever words you want," she babbled. The flashing lights of the police cars were visible. "What are you waiting for...blood? My American Express card?"

He opened the back door of the car and grabbed her stepladder of all things.

"I want you to realize that you need to be rescued and I'm the one who's doing the rescuing." With that, he heaved the ladder over the wall, belatedly calling out, "Heads up!"

Kate opened the ladder just enough to support her weight and scrambled to the top of the wall.

Growling and panting, the dogs flung themselves toward her.

Kate didn't wait to see how far they could jump. She blindly pushed off the wall and braced herself for the landing.

"I've got you," she heard just before falling into the arms of her rescuer.

Her momentum carried them to the road's packed dirt shoulder and when Kate opened her eyes, it was to find herself sprawled on top of her camera, lenses and a warm male body.

He winced and she pulled her equipment out of the way.

"Are you okay?" he asked, his hands moving over her back and arms.

Kate stared into his eyes, a colorless gray-blue with black centers. They reminded her of a camera lens. "Uh..." She must've had the wind knocked out of her.

"Can you run to the car?"

Recalled to the present by his question, Kate registered the approaching sirens and rolled off him, tangling herself in her camera straps.

The man grasped her arm and jerked her to her feet. He crouched and ran.

Instinctively, Kate crouched and ran, too. By the time she opened the passenger door, he'd started the car and put it in gear, flooring the accelerator as soon as she was inside.

Pulling the door shut as they sped away from the villa, Kate swiveled in the seat and watched out the rear window.

"How many cars?" His question was matter-of-fact, as though he'd been in chases before.

"Two at least," she answered as they rounded the corner and began the descent to the coast. "Do you think they'll follow us?"

"Hard to say." He shrugged as if the matter of being pursued by foreign police was of no importance. "It's getting late in the day and we've got a head start."

The car sped onward, passing her rental car, still parked where she'd left it. He navigated two more turns before adding, "I doubt they'll bother." She sensed him glance toward her. "A high-speed chase would upset the tourists."

And this was definitely a high-speed chase. Kate stared at the road behind them and realized he'd guessed correctly. The police weren't following them.

She exhaled in a silent whistle and turned back around.

"Safe at last?" he asked, amusement tinging his words.

"It appears so," she agreed, in relief.

He zoomed the little car onward, swaying perilously close to the cliff side of the road. Kate grabbed for the seat belt, then stopped.

Safe? She stared at the man.

In spite of the winding, narrow road and the speed at which they traveled, he drove one-handed, negligently leaning an elbow on the open window. Upturned cuffs revealed dark hair shading his forearms and two scars— one old and one not so old.

She followed the length of his arms to his neck and the hair curling over his open shirt collar. Squint lines radiated from the corners of his eyes and his skin had a windburned appearance that told her he spent his days out of doors.

As she studied him, he removed his gaze from the road and sent her a slow, enigmatic look that asked nothing and told her nothing, then turned his profile to her once again.

Safe?

Kate held the end of the seat belt without fastening it.

"Thanks," she said into the silence.

He inclined his head.

Oookay. Kate shifted her weight to the balls of her feet and tried to change the end of the seat belt from one hand to the other. "I think we can turn around and go back for my car now," she suggested. "You could pull into one of these scenic spots for tourists and turn around.'' She breathed easier as a sign came into view. ''There's one just ahead.''

Conscious that she sounded too eager, Kate didn't look at him.

The car didn't slow. Was he going to peel in and spin around to impress her? Why did men think women were impressed by that sort of childish—

They passed the scenic overlook.

''Hey!''

He glanced toward her. ''Fasten your seat belt.'' The engine hummed louder.

Did he deliberately misunderstand her? ''Stop the car and let me out.'' Calm and distinct, with an edge of authority. Kate was proud of herself.

He checked his watch and shook his head. ''No time.''

''Well, make time!'' she demanded, forgetting all about calm authority.

The speedometer crept upward.

Kate's seat belt snapped back to the side. An abduction. She was being abducted. ''Just let me out. I'll walk back. No questions.'' Normally, Kate didn't succumb to hysteria so early in a crisis. Leftover adrenaline from the dogs and the police, she supposed. And speaking of police, what was the matter with them? Why hadn't they followed? Couldn't they recognize a kidnapping when they saw one in progress? Didn't they see him *drag* her to the car?

She had no intention of being a cooperative victim. ''Fine! Don't stop the car. *Ciao*!''

She had her hand on the door handle when he grabbed her camera strap, forming an effective noose. The car swayed.

''Kate, stop being an idiot and put on your seat belt!''

CHAPTER TWO

"You know who I am?"

"*Take your hand off the door and put on your seat belt!*"

She ignored him and jerked at her camera. The car veered off the road into the brush and he was forced to let go of the camera strap to regain control.

The guardrail rushed by so close, Kate could see the rust around the bolts.

She gasped.

Within seconds, he'd maneuvered back onto the road. Nodding to her white-knuckled grip on the dashboard, he snapped, "So you're not so eager to fling yourself over the cliff."

She yanked her gaze away from the jagged rocks. "I don't know." She relaxed her grip and edged away from him. "Who are you and where are you taking me?"

"Max Hunter," he replied, without moving his gaze from the curving road.

"Max Hunter," she repeated, her voice flat. She wished he'd looked at her, so she could read his eyes. "As in *Maxwell* Hunter?"

He shrugged. "If you insist."

"*The* Maxwell Hunter?" Just how gullible did he think she was? "Famed and much-lauded, Pulitzer-prize-winning Maxwell Hunter?"

"You're not impressed," he said.

"Oh, I'm impressed." She crossed her arms over her chest.

"You don't sound like it."

"I'm impressed at how *stupid* you think I am."

He grinned, showing even teeth.

Kate made a disgusted sound and surveyed the passing terrain for escape opportunities. Not many presented themselves.

"Don't be so hard on yourself. I probably would've gone for the wall, too."

Kate blinked, trying to follow his sequence of thought, then slowly turned to face him and blinked again. "Are you implying that climbing the wall to get away from the dogs was *stupid*?"

"Of course it was stupid," he said, as if no one in her right mind would dare argue.

Except Kate. "Being eaten would have been even *stupider*."

"You got trapped in the gardens," he pointed out.

The car took the next turn a wee bit fast. Kate clung to the edge of her seat, but refused to fasten the seat belt. "I couldn't *know* that."

"I was standing right there," he said. "I *told* you not to go over the wall."

"Well, excuse me for not instantly obeying the commands of a complete stranger."

He glared at her, then exhaled, gripping the steering wheel. She'd annoyed him, that was obvious. He sighed again, then said, "Let's start over. Hi, I'm Max Hunter."

She rolled her eyes. "Can't you pick another name?"

"You're supposed to say, 'I'm Kate Brandon. Pleased to meet you,'" he prompted her.

"But I'm not."

The car slowed as he downshifted to take another curve. "You're not Kate Brandon?" He looked so disconcerted, that Kate was tempted to deny it. But, if he were kidnapping Kate Brandon and thought she was someone else, then she'd be of no further use to him.

He was probably preparing to throw her over the cliffs right now.

"I'm not pleased to meet you," she clarified.

The car resumed its breakneck speed.

"You don't believe I'm Max Hunter, is that it?"

Because if you did believe I'm Max Hunter, you'd be thrilled to meet me, Kate supplied silently. "That's it."

"Why shouldn't I be Max Hunter?"

"Has Capri declared war on anyone?"

He laughed. "No."

"Maxwell Hunter photographs wars."

His jaw tensed and all expression disappeared from his face. Ah, she'd hit a sore spot. "Maybe he's tired of photographing wars."

The man who called himself Max had spoken in a voice that sounded flat and dead. Tired. Burned out. For the first time, Kate considered that he might actually *be* Maxwell Hunter. She tried to remember. Hadn't she read something about him retiring? Quitting?

What had happened? Maybe she'd get the opportunity to ask.

As she studied him, he nodded to the back seat. "My passport's in my coat pocket."

As if a passport couldn't be forged. Kate obliged him by rummaging through the clutter in the back until she unearthed his jacket. It was a battered brown that smelled of leather, outdoors and men's grooming scents.

She located the passport, which looked genuine enough. It was thick, with extra pages stamped with the entry and exit visas of an impressive array of countries.

"Oh, my God!"

He winced. "My picture's not that bad, is it?"

Kate glared at him. "You're only thirty-four?"

She caught him checking his reflection in the rearview mirror. "Yeah," he admitted defensively.

"The legendary Maxwell Hunter can't be just thirty-four." Only four years older than she was, but look what he'd achieved. Awards. Fame. Recognition. Money.

Respect.

"How old did you think I was?"

"I didn't think about it." She *wouldn't* think about it.

"Think now."

Smothering a smile at this glimpse of vanity, she searched his dark head for a hint of gray, his jawline for sag, his belly for a paunch. Remembering the feel of him beneath her when she fell, she mentally scratched the last. There was no paunch anywhere on this man.

Man. Suddenly, Kate was looking at him as a man, not as her rescuer or as the instrument of her abduction. He was...attractive. Not movie-star handsome like Damian, but his features would pass for good-looking in any culture.

And probably had.

"You look about forty-five," she said to needle him.

"I feel forty-five," he muttered. "No...I feel a hundred and forty-five."

He glanced at her and the passport she held before staring out the windshield again. Kate hoped he was concentrating on driving and not memories.

That brief collision with his gray eyes had chilled her. *They'd* seen enough for a hundred and forty-five years.

"So," she said, tossing the passport in the back. "Where is the great Maxwell Hunter taking me?" *And what is he doing here in the first place?*

For a minute, she thought he wasn't going to answer her. Her heart, which hadn't slowed to normal the entire time she'd been with him, picked up speed.

He sighed. "Think you could manage to call me Max without any adjectives?"

Humor the man. "Where are we going, Max?" she asked in a sweet singsong.

"To the marina, Kate."

"Why is that, Max?"

"To catch Fiona and Damian, Kate."

She gasped. "You know about them?"

As he nodded, another thought occurred to her. "And you care?"

"*Care* isn't the right word. I'm just doing a favor for a friend."

Kate narrowed her eyes. "Who's your friend?"

"Glen Hedgecoe."

Her editor at *World Eye*. "You and Glen know each other?"

"We worked together once upon a time. Hasn't Glen told you stories of his wild and woolly youth?"

Yes, but she hadn't paid attention. "So our meeting isn't just a coincidence?"

"You *did* tell him you were staking out the villa."

And that would be the last time Kate would leave herself open to the competition. Of course, she hoped this would be the last time she had to work for Glen, period. Glen had turned *World Eye* into a publication Kate didn't want to be associated with anymore. She clamped her teeth together and turned away. "You expect me to believe that the exalted Maxwell—"

"Please, no adjectives."

"Tell me you *aren't* free-lancing for *World Eye*."

"Just this once."

Kate absorbed the implications. Even free-lancing for the same tabloid, the fact that they both were trying for pictures of the two stars meant that she was competing against the famous Maxwell Hunter. Why, she didn't know. The only reason she could fathom was that her complaints about *World Eye*'s increasing vulgarity had made Glen nervous that she'd take her pictures elsewhere. He needn't worry. She'd promised him first crack at any pictures and she intended to keep her word.

In the meantime, Maxwell Hunter needed to understand a few things. "Fiona Ferguson is mine. Glen knows that."

"Glen knows this is a hot story and wants pictures," he replied, confirming Kate's suspicions. "I'm insurance."

Overkill, she thought. The man had a whole wall full of photojournalism awards. "How'd Glen talk you into this?"

"Does it matter?"

Yes, it mattered. It appeared that a picture of Fiona with Damian was worth more than she'd thought and even though money wasn't her primary motive, it was an important consideration.

Kate shot Max a cool look and checked her equipment. They'd arrive at the marina in a few minutes. She scanned the docks for a likely yacht. Surely Fiona and Damian didn't plan to take the public ferry back to Sorrento, although there weren't any throngs of adoring fans about.

Kate's frustration mounted. No other photographers were milling around the marina, either. If she could get a picture, she'd have a guaranteed exclusive. That is, if Max kept his hands on the wheel and not on his camera.

She still wasn't sure exactly what his role in all this was, but she *was* sure that if both of them had pictures of Fiona and Damian, the price would plummet.

"Do you see them?" Max slowed the car as they headed toward the docks.

"No."

He muttered something under his breath.

"What? Did you think they'd be standing on deck waving flags or something?" Kate studied the cars, searching for the one that had driven Fiona and Damian away from the villa.

"No, but I'd hoped you'd be more helpful so Glen will get his picture."

"Glen will get his picture." She watched Max's reflection in the window. "Doesn't he always?"

Max shrugged. "I've no idea."

"If *I'm* the photographer, he does." Whatever Glen's arrangement with Max was, Kate wanted him to know that she still considered this her exclusive assignment until Glen told her otherwise.

The road they traveled on intersected with the main road running along the docks, requiring that they turn. "Which way?" Max asked.

Kate bit her lip. "Right."

"Any particular reason?"

He'd already made the turn before Kate admitted, "Just a hunch." The priciest of the private cruisers were in that direction and Fiona did love her creature comforts.

"Hunches are good. I—"

"Stop," Kate ordered suddenly. "I recognize that car. It's exactly like the one they drove away in."

Max instantly pulled their car off the road, parking opposite the dock. Anchored in the slip was a gleaming white vessel. It looked new and expensive.

"Now who does that belong to?" Kate wondered, positioning her camera with its heavy telephoto lens on the dashboard and squinting through the viewfinder.

"Probably the same person who owns the villa." Max's voice held an edge.

Kate looked up questioningly.

"Claudio Amini," Max supplied.

Claudio Amini. Whispered to walk both sides of the law. Kate had run across him at several Hollywood parties. Grimacing, she returned to her viewfinder. "Fiona has friends in low places."

"Or Damian does."

Outwardly nonchalant, Kate shivered inside. Trespassing on the grounds of the Amini villa. No wonder the police had responded so rapidly. She owed Max. A lot.

"Something's going on," she announced.

Motors grumbled to life. Crewmen cast off. A flash of red appeared briefly in one of the cabin windows.

"Did you see that?" she asked.

"What?" Max rested his arms across the steering wheel. His camera remained in the back seat.

"It looked like Fiona's hair. Come on, you two," Kate crooned. "Wouldn't you like to watch from the deck?"

But as the craft pulled away, no one appeared. Kate sighed, but kept her camera trained on the cruiser. "She's become smarter."

The sound of the motor faded, until all that was left was the slurp of the wake.

"I don't suppose you want to drive past any more boat slips?" Max asked.

"No." Kate screwed on her lens cap and nodded toward the car. A man approached it and got in. "I recognize the driver." She glanced at Max to find him watching her. "They got away."

"Probably." He didn't seem perturbed. Crooking his leg and shifting to face her, Max steepled his hands and peered at her over the fingertips.

Kate felt like a lab specimen and didn't like it. She also wasn't sure she liked Maxwell Hunter, with or without adjectives.

She certainly didn't trust him.

However . . . "Have you got the time to drive me back to my car now?"

"Have the rental agency pick it up."

But that will cost more, Kate just stopped herself from blurting out. She believed in judicious spending. She was a generous tipper, which had paid off in information more than once, but wasting money hurt her thrifty soul. She didn't choose to reveal this about herself to Max, so she only nodded. "Well, then, how about a lift to my hotel?"

"What are you going to do now?"

Those gray eyes of his bothered her. He rarely blinked. "Why do you want to know?" she asked.

"I saved your life this afternoon," he said, his expression partially hidden by his fingertips. "I suppose I feel a lingering responsibility."

"You have an exaggerated sense of responsibility," she scoffed, even as a sudden vivid memory of the snarling dogs flashed through her mind. "But I appreciate your help anyway."

He barely nodded.

Kate checked her watch, without appearing to do so. The public ferry—the last one of the day—left in forty-five minutes. She intended to be on it.

Without Maxwell Hunter.

Time to get going. "See you around," she said with all the false sincerity she could muster and shoved open the door.

Instantly, the car motor roared into life. "I'll drive you to your hotel."

She hadn't even heard Max move. She'd remember that.

Although she was desperately short of time, Kate hesitated, the door open. She didn't trust Max to drive her to her hotel and even if he did, she didn't want him to know she planned to catch the last ferry without him. She wanted full and sole credit for any pictures of Fiona and Damian.

Max shifted the car into gear. "Kate."

Her name was a command and she responded by slamming the door shut. He'd better not get the idea that he could boss her around. She'd had enough of that growing up with four brothers and sisters.

They sped through the marina area as Kate silently fussed and fumed. They'd turned onto the street where her modest hotel was located before it occurred to her that she hadn't told Max where she was staying. Glen didn't even know where she was staying.

This man was good.

Shaken, she thanked him politely and scrambled out of the car. She knew he watched her run up the steps and couldn't resist turning around for a last look.

He wore the same self-satisfied smirk he'd worn when he'd leaned against his car outside the villa's front gate.

Kate continued running up the three flights of stairs to her room. This was all a game to Maxwell Hunter. He was toying with her, amusing himself in his retirement. How he'd hooked up with Glen Hedgecoe, she couldn't imagine.

Wait a minute... Glen occasionally referred to his time in the "trenches." Kate had never dreamed he meant literally. Could he have been a war correspondent with Maxwell Hunter? Was that when they'd worked together? Or were they really just friends?

Friends? No. Impossible. The two men couldn't be more different. Glen with his pale, freckled skin and thinning, sandy red hair and Max.

Max. A swarthy observer with overcast eyes, a lean body and a detached attitude. Glen, the endomorph with a temper.

Kate shivered, grabbed her duffel bag and checked under the bed. It was a ritual. She rarely unpacked more than she needed for the day, so there was nothing that could slide under the bed. Her cosmetic bag rested on the floor by the brown-stained sink and a packet of batteries and film sat on the dresser.

Nothing fancy, but Kate couldn't justify spending money for a room in which she did nothing but sleep—and sometimes precious little of that.

Moments after zipping her duffel and hauling it on her already overburdened shoulders, she settled her bill with the front desk and made peace with the car rental company.

Half an hour until the ferry departed and it was no more than a fifteen-minute stroll to the landing.

Kate, with a glance left and right up the pebbled street, set off.

She'd half expected to see Max waiting for her and examined every car that went past.

She didn't want to think about Max. She didn't want to work with anyone, even the great Maxwell Hunter. Or just plain Max. She worked alone. She always had.

Once she reached Sorrento, Kate vowed, she'd call Glen and reverse the charges. Cracking a smile, she imagined him waking up in the middle of the night and paying for the privilege.

And then she heard the voices. Many voices. Excited voices.

Kate stopped just before reaching the marina road and the ferry station. Sliding along a building wall, she peeked around it.

A crowd.

Smacking the wall with her fist, Kate leaned against it and closed her eyes. Great. Fiona and Damian must be taking the public ferry after all. Fans and paparazzi everywhere.

Kate caught snatches of babble in several languages before realizing that the people were angry, not excited.

Checking the crowd more carefully, she saw no photographers—at least no professional ones. She did see luggage and sunburn and unattractive hats.

Tourists. It was a tour group and not Fiona playing superstar. Exhaling in relief, Kate went to buy her ticket, automatically looking around for Max. She didn't see him.

"No tickets," announced the woman behind the glass window.

"There have to be tickets," Kate insisted.

The woman pointed. "They bought them all."

"The tour group?"

"Two." The woman held up two fingers. "For the same crossing. Very bad mix-up."

Whirling around, Kate identified two angry tour operators apparently fighting over which group would board the ferry. There obviously wasn't room for everyone. "Well, the ferry will have to make another trip, right?"

The woman shrugged. "No more tickets."

This was absurd. "How am I going to get to Sorrento?" Kate asked.

"Tomorrow."

"But I have to leave now!" Kate shouted as the woman sat back in her chair and turned to a tiny television.

Muttering, Kate left the window.

The crowd raptly watched three men argue. The tour operators had found the ferry captain and were both talking and gesturing at once.

Kate slipped into the crowd. One of the groups would eventually triumph and Kate intended to mingle with the winner.

The ferry captain tapped his watch and crossed his arms, obviously unconcerned.

A few people boarded, defiantly planting themselves on the chairs.

The tour operators shouted and pointed, and at last, the ferry captain held up both hands, palms outward, and stalked off.

"Oh, terrific!" Kate snarled, pushed her way out of the tourists and prepared to follow the ferry captain into a dockside tavern.

"Going my way?"

The sound of the mildly amused male voice brought Kate up short. Max lounged on the wooden benches outside the ticket office, looking as though he'd enjoyed the spectacle.

"No one is going anywhere." Kate hesitated, then sat beside him. "Apparently two gigantic tour groups hold tickets for the same ferry crossing and they're arguing over who will get to board." Hooking her foot through her duffel strap she grumbled, "Now the captain's mad."

"He'll get over it."

"Yeah, but when?"

"You're right. It hardly matters. By then—" Max paused to stretch his arms "—Fiona and Damian will be long gone."

Kate slumped on the bench.

Max crossed his legs at the ankles, fostering the impression of a man without a care in the world. "You don't impress me as the sort of woman who'd let a little thing like a sold-out ferry stop her."

Kate gestured to the tourists. "When the ferry starts running again—and who knows when that will be?—

you *know* the captain will board whichever tour operator bribes him the most. All the others will fend for themselves.''

Max clicked his tongue. ''Kate, Kate, Kate. So cynical. So unimaginative.''

The cynical part was true, but the unimaginative crack stung. ''What do you mean?'' She straightened. ''It took imagination to track down Fiona and Damian. Even to figure out that there was something to track down.''

''Dare I point out that the knowledge isn't doing you any good at this precise moment?'' He smiled contentedly, leaned his head back and closed his eyes.

She glared at him, then turned her gaze toward the marina. ''I'll catch up with them,'' she muttered, mostly to herself. ''Sooner or later, she's bound to slip up.''

''You surprise me, Kate.''

She ignored him.

''You triumphed over dogs, walls and the police only to let a mere ferry stop you.''

Uncomfortable, Kate remembered that the only reason she'd ''triumphed'' over anything was due to his help. ''You seem to be letting it stop you,'' she said. *Hey, Glen, your big gun ran out of ammo.*

''Not at all.''

She didn't have to look at him to know that his mouth was set in the smug, almost-smile expression she was beginning to hate.

''What did you do, book yourself on each of the tours?'' That was Kate's own last-ditch plan.

''No, I booked a boat.''

Her mouth dropped open, but fortunately his eyes were still shut, so he missed her expression. ''You hired a boat?''

''It seemed to be the only way.''

How big a boat? He'd said boat, not yacht. Kate's breathing quickened. "Then why aren't you on it?"

"The captain's refueling."

Involuntarily, she scanned the marina.

"That one." Max opened one eye and pointed. "Over there."

A little cabin cruiser. Plenty of room, unless other stranded people had thought of the same thing. Kate's grip tightened on her camera strap. "Did you, uh, hire the whole thing or just buy yourself passage?"

Max rubbed his upper lip. "The whole thing."

He was toying with her, just as he'd toyed with her when he'd stood outside the gates at the Amini villa.

Kate swallowed and noticed that both Max's eyes were open now and watching her. They stared at each other, surrounded by the stranded tourists, indifferent dockworkers and the glorious blue waters of the Mediterranean—the same blue waters keeping Kate stuck on Capri.

Max was waiting for her to ask him for a ride back to Sorrento, she knew. For some probably male reason, it appeared important to him that she ask.

And it was just as important for her not to ask.

But was it important enough to miss the chance to catch Fiona and Damian?

Her gaze shifted from his watchful, colorless eyes to the boat.

"Looks like he's just about ready." Max stretched indolently and prepared to stand. "Time to shove off."

"Are you going to offer me a ride?" she asked quietly.

"No."

It was as she suspected then. Nothing less than a formal request would suffice. "May I have a ride back to Sorrento?"

"Yes." He reached down, untangled her duffel strap, hooked the bag across his shoulder and held out his hand.

At that moment, Kate loathed the brilliant Maxwell Hunter. She slipped her hand in his, releasing it as soon as she was on her feet.

"What will this cost me?" She wasn't asking about the monetary cost, although naturally, she'd offer. But a man who casually hired a boat didn't have to worry about money.

His gray eyes regarded her unblinkingly and the corner of his mouth pulled upward in the barest of smiles. "We'll negotiate...later."

CHAPTER THREE

KATE and Max's boat skimmed toward the Sorrento marina, arriving well ahead of the ferry, but well behind Fiona and Damian, not that Kate had held out any hope of finding the two lovebirds lingering on the docks.

Spotting the gleaming cruiser rocking gently in the slip, Kate plotted her next move, even as she was aware of Max's relaxed stance at the helm of the boat. Obviously, he hadn't expected to catch up with Fiona and Damian, either. In fact, he acted as though he hadn't a care in the world. He'd spent the trip chatting easily with the captain or gripping the railing, smiling as the wind and spray tore through his hair.

Easy for *him* to smile, Kate thought grumpily, mentally tallying her dwindling lira as their boat docked. Could she afford another few days here in Italy? She'd just have to, since she'd already invested so much time and money on this project.

Besides, now that Max was involved, capturing Fiona and Damian on film had become a matter of pride.

"*Arrivederci*!" Max waved to the captain and turned to Kate, prompting her with a raised brow.

Taking the hint, Kate smiled and nodded as she grabbed her duffel bag and stepped onto the weathered wood of the dock. How much did she owe for her passage? And when should she settle her account?

"Here we are," Max announced with a cheeriness Kate felt was unwarranted.

She started to make a snappy remark at him, but the words died on her lips.

Something had happened to Max on that boat ride. It was as if the sea and salt had scoured years off his face.

Or it could be that the gentle Italian twilight was particularly flattering. Very flattering.

The burnished glow that had inspired centuries of painters now inspired Kate. Impulsively, she dropped her duffel on the dock and snapped open her camera. The picture would require a long exposure in this light and was likely to be jittery since she wouldn't be using a tripod, but Kate didn't care. She wanted to capture the great Maxwell Hunter as he looked right now—carefree, amused, relaxed.

And very attractive.

"What?" He swiveled his head at the sound of her camera. "You haven't seen our quarry, have you?"

"No." Kate set the exposure. When he turned his head to look at her, she was ready and managed one click of the shutter.

"Why did you do that?" he asked with a laugh. "Am I looking particularly ghoulish right now?" He finger combed his windswept hair as Kate considered her reply.

"You look happy." Now that she couldn't catch him unaware, she replaced her lens cap. "And I think," she added slowly, wondering if she should, "that you haven't been happy in a while."

He regarded her for a moment, then swept his gaze toward the bay. The golden light warmed his face, but didn't reach his eyes. "The last time I was in a boat was February, two years ago. Straits of Al-Jimah—at night. Each of us held a spotlight trained on the water. I didn't dare blink. My eyes teared and I was scared to wipe the tears away in case I missed a floating mine marker. And it was cold...so very cold...." His voice trailed off as he remembered.

Kate wanted to ask why he'd been forced to make a dangerous trip in the dark, but sensed that Max wouldn't appreciate her intruding on his memories.

He turned back to face her. "This trip is different."

"I'll say." She slung her equipment over one shoulder. "I'd also say that you've traveled through more mined waters than not." And if she wasn't careful, she could be headed for mined waters herself, where he was concerned.

They stared at each other. The tantalizing glimpse into his past had Kate half-hoping Max would tell her more of his experiences. She knew he was still thinking about them, but he only gave her a brief smile and stooped to pick up his leather backpack by one well-worn strap. "Hungry?" he asked.

"Famished," she admitted, allowing him to change the subject without argument.

He glanced at his watch and then, his hand resting in the small of her back, nudged her toward the outdoor tables of a tiny *trattoria*. "We've got about forty minutes until our train leaves."

"Train?" Kate stopped walking.

Max dropped his arm. "You're headed for Rome next, aren't you?"

"Yes, but I haven't made any arrangements yet."

"I have," Max informed her and strode toward the chipped metal tables.

Kate trotted behind him. "What arrangements have you made?"

Max dropped his backpack and pulled out a wobbly chair for her, scraping it over the cement. "I've got two tickets on the nine o'clock train to Rome." He sat back in the chair opposite and guilelessly looked up at her. "That *is* where Fiona and Damian are filming."

Kate felt manipulated and didn't like it. "And you just *assumed* I'd want to come along with you?"

"Don't you?"

Not on principle, but she'd be foolish to let pride interfere with her work. Wordlessly, she sat at the table and snatched at the greasy handwritten menu. "How did you get the tickets already?"

Grinning, Max gave the menu a quick once-over. "I called from the ferry office on Capri."

Remembering the uncooperative woman in front of her tiny television, Kate scowled. She should have thought of calling ahead herself.

"What's the matter?"

"You're awfully competent for a beginner," she said and closed the menu.

Max chuckled and signaled for a waiter. "I'm hardly a beginner."

"You are at this."

"You'd be annoyed if I weren't any help at all. In fact, you'd have left me on Capri, wouldn't you?"

She tossed the menu in front of her. "It's not my policy to help the competition."

"I'm not competition," he said easily.

"Then what are you?" *Let's have it out right now.*

"Let's say I'm an interested party."

"Let's not." She fixed him with an intent gaze, trying to see into his eyes and read his motives.

He returned her gaze, his expression as closed and as unyielding as she tried to make her own.

They were two of a kind—both loners who didn't reveal themselves to people. They observed and recorded human nature and didn't like it when they were scrutinized by others. In Max, Kate recognized a kindred soul.

"Okay." He lifted a shoulder as if her suspicions were of no concern to him. "I suppose you've heard that I retired as a photojournalist."

Kate noticed that he didn't say "quit". She lifted her shoulder and duplicated his I-don't-care gesture.

For a moment, she thought she saw a flash of annoyance in his expression, but he masked it quickly. "I'm exploring new directions. Your job appeals to me."

She swallowed. "That's blunt."

"I don't mean your arrangement with Glen's paper," he was quick to reassure her, "but the idea of photographing celebrities."

"As you've no doubt guessed, the idea is much more glamorous than the reality," Kate said as a waiter appeared.

"I'm sure it is," Max agreed, and ordered two pizzas. "Unless you'd prefer something else?" he thought to ask.

How did he know she was going to order pizza? Italian pizza wasn't even like the gooey cheese-laden American pizza. For all he knew, she hated thick pizzas. But she didn't and why should she change the order just to prove him wrong? "That'll be fine," she said with a tight smile. Did he have to be right about *everything*?

"Glen said you were one of the best."

He had? Kate filed this information away to use in negotiating payment with Glen for this final set of pictures.

Max poured mineral water into a glass and gave it to her. "You don't mind offering a colleague a few pointers, do you?"

Kate did mind. Very much. However... Max was flattering her and it was proving effective. Maxwell Hunter considered her a colleague? *Asked* her for pointers? Pretty heady stuff.

"What do you want to know?" she asked, avoiding a direct answer.

"This is fairly much an anything-goes field, right?"

"Meaning . . . ?"

"Meaning you make your own rules."

Max's eyes were bright—as bright as gray eyes could get. Kate guessed that the idea of following no rules but his own appealed to him.

After all, didn't that appeal to her?

"So what do you want?" she asked, again avoiding a direct answer.

He leaned forward. "Let me tag along with you."

That was *not* a good idea, but Kate knew she had no choice. If she refused his request, Max was the type to scoop her just to prove he could do it. Better to acquiesce. At least she'd know where he was.

But first, she'd set some ground rules—her rules. "As long as you understand that this is *my* assignment and we do it *my* way."

He tensed. After a moment, he inclined his head. "All right." It was obvious that Maxwell Hunter was used to being in charge. Kate felt she'd won an important victory.

The pizza took longer to prepare than they'd expected. After eating a couple of pieces, they wrapped the rest, grabbed their bottled water and jogged to the train, managing to pick up their tickets—first class—and hop on board with just minutes to spare.

They sat across from each other, still breathing heavily as the train rolled out of the station.

"Made it." Max looked pleased with himself.

"Just." Kate managed a tired smile back at him and peeled the grease-soaked paper napkin from her pizza. "Now is a good time to settle our finances." She tore off a piece of the lukewarm pizza and stuffed it into her mouth, afraid she was about to lose her appetite. This trip might not be as profitable as she'd hoped.

"Don't worry about it." Max eyed his paper-wrapped bundle with distaste, and set it on the seat beside him.

But of course Kate would worry until she knew the precise amount of her debt. She swallowed with difficulty. "Expenses were that much?" She tried for a casual tone, but his knowing look told her she hadn't succeeded.

"I only meant that I'll put everything on my expense report. It'll be easier."

Kate zeroed in on two words. "You've got an expense account?"

"You better believe it."

"Glen Hedgecoe is paying your expenses?" she asked sharply. The most she'd been able to wangle out of Glen had been advance money for her airplane ticket—and that he planned to deduct from what he'd pay her for her picture.

Max hesitated and Kate realized that she'd revealed more about herself than she'd intended to.

"It's...usually customary when I accept an assignment," he informed her lightly.

"Not with Glen." That cheap, chiseling rat. The price of a Fiona Ferguson photograph just went up.

"Have you ever asked for expenses?"

"*Of course!*" Kate snapped and, embarrassed, took a huge bite of now-cold pizza. Here she was, in the presence of one of the all-time great photojournalists and she was coming off like a naive, incompetent amateur.

Well, maybe she was.

Max toyed with the bottle of water, taking a sip. "You could always sell your pictures elsewhere."

"I could." And she intended to—other pictures. Kate stared at her hands. They were shiny with grease and she dug in her pockets for a tissue. "But I've found that only staff photographers—and famous photojournalists—get expenses. Free-lancers are on their own." She couldn't find a tissue and settled for lens-cleaning papers.

"Why haven't you signed on as a staff photographer?" Max asked.

"Glen hasn't offered me the position." And she wouldn't take it now if he did; not as long as *World Eye* continued its emphasis on lurid stories instead of real news. She wasn't going to tell Max that, though.

"Did you ask him?"

Kate nodded. "A while back. He claims that *World Eye* can't afford it. And frankly, I never know if his checks are going to bounce or not."

"How long have you been putting up with this?" Max asked.

"Several months." More than several. "Over a year," Kate corrected, then realized it was closer to two years. *Two years.* She was too embarrassed to admit that to Max.

"I kept thinking things would change," she defended herself when he raised an eyebrow. "And some months, sales climbed, then they'd fall again."

Smut sells, Glen would preach. Unfortunately he appeared to be right and paid her accordingly.

Kate sighed. She had to get out. She had to. And she would. Fiona was going to be her ticket out.

Max apparently caught her sigh. "Why've you stuck with him so long?"

Why *had* she? "I . . . loyalty, I guess. He gave me my first big sale back when I really needed the money."

"And you don't need money now?"

Kate smiled ruefully. "Good point."

At that, he smiled, too. "It's easy to get into a rut. It's also easy to underestimate your value."

"Or to price yourself out of the market," Kate warned him.

"Sometimes you've got to take chances."

That's easy to say when you've got a fat bank account, Kate thought. Which was one reason she wanted this picture. "Thanks for the advice."

He gestured negligently. "Think nothing of it."

"I will."

Max laughed, a loud, robust laugh that went on for too long. "You don't like me, do you?"

Did being attracted to him count? "I hardly know you and what I do know threatens my financial well-being."

"I'm no threat. Believe me."

"Why should I?"

His face hardened. "Because I could have left you to the dogs, left you on Capri or left you in Sorrento."

"Why didn't you?"

Something flared in his eyes. He didn't answer immediately, and Kate suspected he was carefully selecting his response. "I've been known to help out when a fellow photographer's in trouble."

"This may be a shock, but I'm not completely helpless. I had a plan for leaving Capri."

Max's face told her what he thought of her plan. "And then what?"

"Then I would have gone to Rome."

"You're on your way to Rome now."

"So I am."

Kate closed her eyes and leaned her head back, relaxing to the sway of the train and the monotonous rush of sound. She didn't want to think about arriving in Rome in the dead of night. Why worry? Max obviously wasn't.

Maxwell Hunter. Infuriating and compelling at the same time, the man fascinated her. She peeked at him through her lashes, only to find him watching her without a trace of expression.

Max. She couldn't figure the man out and the fact that she wanted to should have set alarm bells clanging.

The fact that it didn't should have been warning enough. For now though, she'd try to sleep.

Goodness knows, she was probably in for a lot of sleepless nights in the future.

"Don't be stubborn, Kate." Max hailed a taxi outside the train station. "I've already made reservations for us at the Principe."

A hotel that did not appear in her *Budget Guide to Rome.* "Thanks, but I prefer the Villa de San Marco." It was time to make a stand. Time to regain control. Time to stop allowing Max to make all the arrangements, convenient though it was.

"The Principe is a wonderful hotel. I know the concierge."

It figured.

"Come on." He picked up her duffel bag. "It'll be a treat for you."

Meaning it was very expensive. Kate was torn between allowing herself the "treat" knowing Glen would pay for it, and breaking this pattern of Kate, the incompetent, and Max, the white knight.

Still not certain of their final destination, she climbed into the taxi.

On one hand, it *was* the wee hours of the night and Kate had never stayed in a hotel the caliber of the Principe. On the other, she wanted Max to think well of her, though she'd be hard put to explain how staying in the Villa de San Marco would gain his respect.

She hadn't made reservations at the Villa. It was so easy to rationalize doing something she wanted to do anyway.

Kate did have qualms as she entered the marbled foyer of the grand hotel.

Max was greeted as an old friend, and Kate, her scruffy appearance reflected in a dozen gilt-edged mirrors, was accorded respect because she was with him.

"Kate," Max said, urging her forward. "I'd like you to meet Signor Giordano, the Principe's concierge."

An elderly gentleman, no taller than she, inclined his head. "Welcome to the Principe, *signorina*."

Kate smiled wanly.

"Kate's an associate of mine," Max said while Kate attempted to maintain her smile. "She needs some of your special coddling."

"Certainly."

Kate felt about twelve years old, but that didn't mean the concept of coddling was repugnant, either.

They squeezed into an ancient elevator and ascended so slowly Kate thought they should have taken the stairs. When the elevator creaked to a stop, she climbed out with relief.

Their footsteps echoed down the marble-floored hallway until Signor Giordano stopped in front of a set of pale blue doors with gold handles. With a flourish, he wielded a heavy brass key and pushed them open, dramatically moving to one side so they could get the full effect.

Max obviously took the effect in stride and was in the living room of the suite before he noticed that Kate had frozen on the threshold.

"Kate?" He turned and gestured for her to come in.

"*Signorina*?" The beginnings of a concerned frown marred the concierge's smiling expression.

"Uh . . ." What could she say? What did she want to say?

Max decided for her. Returning to the doorway, he tugged her inside. "This suite has two bedrooms," he said with the slightest bit of emphasis. "One on this side," he said, pointing, "and the other over here. You pick."

Pick? She gazed around, assaulted by images of mirrors, marble, gilt, paintings and furniture that looked as if they had once lived in a palazzo and probably had. In fact, wasn't the Principe a converted palace?

"May I suggest this bedroom, *signorina*?" the concierge gestured discreetly. "The bath is a *trifle* larger."

"Thank you," Kate said, managing to recover her aplomb. She prided herself on handling any situation.

This, however, was an entirely new situation.

As Kate followed Signor Giordano across the living room and through the dining room, with a long table already set for twelve, she reflected that this hotel suite was bigger than her entire apartment. Furthermore, the tariff for one night would probably pay her rent for a whole month.

When she stepped into the bedroom, Kate couldn't suppress a tiny gasp.

"Is all to your satisfaction, *signorina*?"

Who was he kidding?

The room, from canopied, satin-covered bed to the fireplace in the corner, was like something Kate had only seen in magazine pictures.

And it was useless to pretend that she was accustomed to staying in places like this. She glanced at the concierge, whose eyebrows were drawn together with anxious, eager-to-please concern, and decided to be honest. "I'm overwhelmed," she admitted. "The beauty of this room will feed my soul for days to come."

She was rewarded by a huge smile.

Hurrying to the bathroom, Signor Giordano pointed out the thick towels, turned on the heated towel rack, then twisted the taps on a bathtub that could have doubled as a swimming pool.

He opened a small linen closet and removed a white terry cloth robe with the Principe logo embroidered in pale blue and draped it on the towel rack.

Kate smiled gratefully as the concierge bowed himself out and closed the doors.

This was serious coddling. She studied the selection of bath oils and beads nestled in a white wicker basket, selected a bottle and drizzled a rose fragrance into the tub.

Glen would never pay for such luxurious accommodations, no matter how famous Max was nor how close acquaintances they were.

No doubt Max could afford to absorb the expense of several nights at the Principe, but Kate couldn't.

She turned off the water and heard a tapping.

"Kate?" Max's voice sounded clearly through the door. Apparently, old Italian palazzos weren't sound-proof. "When you get out—"

Since she hadn't yet undressed, Kate opened the door.

"Ah, glad I caught you." Max held out a small silver tray.

"What's this?" A tiny glass filled with amber liquid sat next to a mug of milk.

"You've made a conquest of Signor Giordano." Max touched the liquor. "This is from his private stock and the warm milk is to help you sleep."

Kate smiled. "I don't think I'll need help sleeping." But she took the tray.

"Good night." Max turned to leave.

"Max?"

He stopped, dark brow raised.

Kate wanted to tell him that they couldn't possibly stay here indefinitely. She wanted to warn him of Glen's tightfisted ways. She wanted to let him know that she couldn't afford to repay him, unless she managed to get an extremely incriminating picture of Fiona and Damian. She wanted to define their relationship on this project.

But not in the middle of the night.

"What is it?" he asked, when her silence stretched.

"Thanks," she said at last, cowardly postponing the unpleasantness until the morning.

He nodded. "Sleep well."

Kate stood at the doorway until he'd disappeared into the living room, then looked down at the tray in her hands. Stray water drips from the tub caused her to glance from it to the bed, which Signor Giordano must have turned down before he left.

"Kate," she said aloud and closed the bathroom door, "you might as well enjoy what's left of the night."

She set the tray on the marble counter and took a tiny sip of the liquor, following it with a larger swallow of the milk, its warmth spreading throughout her middle.

This was the life.

She'd just better not get used to it.

CHAPTER FOUR

KATE had planned to have a serious discussion with Max over breakfast, but breakfast arrived at her bedside.

A gentle tap on the door gave her just enough warning to clutch the satin bedclothes to her chest and hide the fact that she was attired in a cotton T-shirt rather than the flowing silk gown the room deserved.

"Has Mr. Hunter eaten yet?" Kate asked the maid who entered.

"I believe he has." The motherly woman set a bed tray over Kate's lap and gently pushed her back against the pillows. "The *signore* said for you to relax."

Kate made only a token protest as the maid quietly closed the door. She had to eat, didn't she? And that orange juice was undoubtedly freshly squeezed....

It was. Pouring herself coffee from the thermal pot, Kate added sugar, then leaned against the pillows, feeling more content than she had a right to feel. The heavy damask draperies blocked out the sunlight so she had no idea what time it was and found that it was too much effort to reach for her watch. Instead, she reached for a piece of toast, glad to see it instead of the hard rolls that seemed to be a staple of Italian life.

On the breakfast tray, there was a folded English-language newspaper, which Kate opened, looking for any information about Fiona's film, *Roman Vengeance*. She didn't really expect to find anything, but had to convince herself she was accomplishing something while lying in the lap of luxury.

The fact that she actually found a two-line blurb in the entertainment section startled her. She was even more startled to read that the location work was nearly completed. Nearly completed? And she still didn't have any incriminating pictures of Fiona and Damian!

Kate splashed coffee in her haste to get out of bed. Had she lost her mind? What was she doing lolling about an expensive hotel room when she should be racing to the *Roman Vengeance* location to find out what was going on?

And what was Max doing?

The maid had told her he'd said to relax.

"I'll just bet he wanted me to relax," Kate muttered and pulled on a fresh pair of black pants and changed her black T-shirt.

Max was probably staking out Fiona and Damian right now—and getting *her* picture. Poaching on *her* assignment. She was so close—how could she let anything or anyone interfere now?

The instant she was dressed, Kate raced into the living room. "Max?"

Silence. And worse, his camera bag wasn't visible.

His bedroom door was closed. Kate ran across the living room and pressed her ear against the door.

More silence.

She knocked, waited two seconds and opened the door. "Max?"

He wasn't there, she saw at a glance. Walking farther into the room, she saw his shaving gear, but not his camera.

Great. Just great. Max and his camera were gone. That could mean only one thing—he was off to photograph Fiona.

How could Kate have been so gullible? Sure, he'd *said* he was looking for pointers, *said* he wanted to tag along, *said* he'd do it her way.

But she wasn't in charge; she never had been. If she'd been in charge, they'd be at the Villa de San Marco right now.

Max had thrown down the gauntlet. He was after Fiona.

Kate would just have to catch her first. She'd studied Fiona; at one time, she'd considered Fiona her friend, but not anymore. Kate knew Fiona better than she knew her own sisters and she knew this business better than Max with his wall full of journalism awards. That should count for something.

Kate packed her things in record time, groaning when she discovered that it was already ten-thirty.

She was courting financial disaster, but that didn't stop her from renting a car and driving into the Roman countryside. She'd sleep in the car tonight, if she had to, but she needed the mobility.

When Kate arrived on the movie site, she fully expected to find Max. Knowing him, he'd probably chartered a helicopter.

She circled the area, didn't see him, and couldn't decide if that was a good sign or not. He was always one or two steps ahead of her, which was stressful as well as annoying.

Not much had changed on the movie set in the week she'd been on Capri. Fiona's dressing trailer was still conveniently parked next to the stand of olive trees, providing shade for the trailer and a hiding place for Kate. She hiked to her favorite stakeout spot among the trees and waited.

And waited.

The Italian sun grew hotter and Kate wished she were wearing white, even though her spot was partially shaded. But white would make her more visible, and after the dog incident, she knew Fiona was looking out for her.

In the distance, she watched extras being positioned for exterior scenes around a stone farmhouse. *Roman Vengeance* was the story of an innocent Italian farm girl—Fiona in a casting stretch—whose family farm and village were taken over by a conglomerate. The villagers send her to Rome to plead their case and she falls in love with the enemy—Damian, perfectly cast, in Kate's opinion.

When the villagers discover this, they destroy Fiona's farmhouse. Obviously, that would be the last scene filmed and it looked like that was the one they were preparing to shoot.

Kate settled back for a long wait.

Lunchtime came and hordes of people milled around the trailers and the sandwich wagon. No one had come and gone from Fiona's trailer and there was no sign of Max. Bored and thirsty, Kate decided to see how close she could get to the lunch tables.

Putting on dark glasses, a baseball cap and an I-belong-here attitude, she abandoned her camera and melted into the food line.

Listening to scraps of conversation around her, Kate tried to determine the shooting schedule for the day. It could be that Fiona and Damian weren't even on call, which would make all her effort a monumental waste of time.

She arrived at the large sandwich basket without learning anything of importance. As she reached for a tray, a man standing on the other side of the table said something to her in Italian.

Kate blinked stupidly and he switched to English. "I have not seen you here before."

Uh-oh. Kate took in the apron with the catering company's name. "I...do camera work." The last thing she'd wanted was to attract attention. She smiled and began piling her tray with sandwiches. "My turn to get lunch for the extras," she explained and moved farther down the line, hoping he wouldn't ask her for identification.

"That's not customary—"

"Today it is." Kate added soft drinks for good measure. "Otherwise, they'll quit and we'll get even further behind schedule." The last was a guess. Movies generally ran behind schedule.

"If that does happen, after my duties here, I am available." Leaning forward, he flashed her a white smile.

He was good-looking, with the light coloring of the Northern Italians. He'd obviously been bitten by the acting bug and thought she had some influence with the movie personnel.

And she'd wanted to remain inconspicuous. "Casting isn't really up to me, but I'll keep you in mind. Ciao," she said brightly and quickly walked away, not paying attention to where she was going. She hoped he wouldn't follow her or call after her.

Kate veered away from the olive trees. She didn't dare return to her stakeout spot until she was certain he wasn't behind her. Dodging people, she ducked around a trailer.

And stumbled into Max strolling from the opposite direction.

"Max!"

"You remember." He steadied her and eyed her sandwich-laden tray. "Work up an appetite?"

Kate ignored his sarcasm. "What are you doing with all your camera junk draped around your neck like that?'' He might as well be carrying a sign telling Fiona that the paparazzi were here.

"My dear, this is hardly junk—"

"Shh!" Kate peered around the corner of the trailer to see if they'd been noticed. When she turned back, Max's expression told her he wasn't in a very good humor.

At this point, whether or not he was angry didn't concern her as much as getting caught. "Come with me before somebody sees you and throws us off the set."

"Don't you mean before somebody sees *you* with all those sandwiches?"

"This is a disguise," she retorted, leading him to the olive trees.

Max refused to hurry. Did he want to get caught? Or did he think his press credentials were still good?

Kate stumbled as the thought occurred to her. His credentials probably *were* still good. That meant that if security caught them, Kate would go and Max could stay.

Luck was apparently with her. Heart pounding, she slipped between the trees and impatiently waited until Max joined her.

"Are you *trying* to get me thrown off the set?" she asked in a furious whisper, thumping the tray down by her camera bag.

"Kate—" he scanned the area they'd just left "—no one is paying us the slightest bit of attention. I hardly think all this skulking about is necessary."

"You're wrong, Mr. Famous Journalist," Kate snapped, reacting to the disparaging tone in his voice. "This isn't like wars where you can go right to the action. In this business, you have to creep up on the action, or it'll run away from you."

He pointed to the tray at her feet. "I don't see any legs on those sandwiches."

Kate ripped off her sunglasses and glared at him. "I was trying to blend in."

Max's mouth twitched, infuriating her.

He still didn't get it. But he would. Yes, he'd get it when *she* nabbed the picture of Fiona and Damian and *he* returned to Glen with nothing but a stack of bills. "How long have you been here?"

"I just arrived." He spoke lightly and added, "I could have been here sooner, if I'd known you were ready to leave."

In spite of her anger, she felt guilty. "When you weren't in the room, I thought you'd already left," she offered by way of explanation. Avoiding his gaze, she sat on the ground.

There was a momentary silence when Kate wished she had enough nerve to read Max's expression.

"Well, I'm here now, just in time for lunch." When she said nothing, he asked, "May I join you? I assume you have enough to share."

"Oh, sure." Not very gracious. She smiled stiffly.

Max sat on the ground beside her. Drawing his knees up, he rested his forearms on them and gazed out on all the movie activity. "I admit, this paparazzi business has turned out to be fun."

"Fun?" Kate bristled.

"Sure. The glamour of the movies, stars, intrigue..." He nodded at her tray. "And, I assume, good food."

Kate tossed him a paper-wrapped bundle, which he caught with one hand.

"Not to mention your scintillating company," he added with a sideways look at her.

Kate was in no mood for banter. She was still embarrassed. Besides, he'd nearly given them away and wasn't concerned at all. "This is all a game to you, isn't it?"

He eyed her thoughtfully as he unwrapped the sandwich. "Do you enjoy all this sneaking around?"

"Not particularly."

"Then why do you do it?"

Because I want to show Jonathan what kind of woman Fiona really is. But Kate didn't want to discuss her brother's broken heart with Max. "I do what it takes to get the job done." She bit into her sandwich, chewing defiantly.

"Ever thought about a different job?"

Kate swallowed, then admitted, "Yes."

Max raised an eyebrow. "And?"

"And what?"

"You're so prickly. I was merely curious about what sort of person becomes a paparazzi."

He sounded vaguely disapproving and Kate responded defensively, "I don't know about others, but I started out as a free-lance feature photographer and illustrator. *World Eye* was a weekly news publication then."

"Was it?" His eyes sparked with interest.

Kate nodded. "But Glen had a hard time competing with magazines. Then one day a story blew up and he had nothing to run on the front page but a huge photo of some celebrity flavor-of-the-month. One of *my* photos."

"Sales took off, right?" Max opened a can of soda.

"Did they ever." Kate grimaced. "Within a year, Glen went completely tabloid. Now all he wants from me are sleazy peekaboo shots of famous people." The candid shots Kate preferred to take weren't racy enough for Glen anymore. And so, she told herself again, after she caught Fiona with Damian, she'd market her pictures elsewhere.

"You don't have to do this." Max must have heard the disgust in her voice. "We can leave right now."

"I..." Kate looked into his eyes and saw the concern. He meant every word and she was grateful. "Thanks, but I promised Glen I'd go after Fiona." Kate craned her neck to see around Fiona's trailer. "Where is she anyway? She didn't go in while we were talking, did she?" Taking a bite of her sandwich, Kate scanned the parking lot.

"No." Max looked at his watch. "I imagine she's just now leaving her hotel."

Kate stopped chewing. "What?" She swallowed.

"She has a three o'clock call today. Something about evening exteriors." He tossed off this information in the same tone of voice one used for discussing the weather.

"How do you know that?" Kate asked, her eyes narrowing.

"Giovanni found out and told me," Max explained and tapped his sandwich. "These are good. I love Italian bread."

Swiveling around until she faced him, Kate demanded, "Who's Giovanni?"

"Giordano," Max clarified. "The concierge. You met him last—"

"*I remember.*"

Max shrugged and reached for another sandwich, which infuriated Kate.

"How can you sit there and eat?"

"There's plenty. Have another."

"I don't want another!"

"If you weren't hungry, why'd you take so many?"

Kate thought she'd explode. Max's innocent expression didn't fool her for an instant. He was enjoying himself—at her expense. He probably thought it was funny that she'd spent hours in the hot sun waiting for Fiona when all the time *he* knew Fiona was back at her hotel.

Which prompted a horrible thought. "Is Fiona staying at the Principe?"

Max shook his head.

That was a relief. It was short-lived. "When did you find all this out?"

"This morning."

"Was...was I there?" Kate plucked at a blade of grass to avoid looking at him.

"You mean, did I know where Fiona was before you disappeared with all your worldly goods?" He spoke lightly, but Kate heard the edge in his voice and knew it rankled that she'd left without telling him.

Darting a glance at him, she nodded, feeling guilty. "You weren't in your room and I wanted to get started," she explained. Her excuse sounded lame even to her.

"You could've left a note or a message. But to answer your question, yes, I awoke early, discovered Fiona's schedule and thought you'd enjoy sleeping in."

Oh. "Thanks, but I wish you'd told me."

"Didn't you get your breakfast?" Annoyance crossed his face.

Kate was momentarily diverted. "Did *you* order breakfast for me?"

"Yes, it was supposed to be breakfast in bed. I thought you deserved a reward after yesterday."

Kate must have looked puzzled because he continued, "Most women would have succumbed to hysteria at least once. You never did." His colorless gaze traced her face and settled on her eyes. "I wanted to thank you for that."

Her emotions unexpectedly jumbled, Kate stared at him. It had been a lovely gesture—or would have been had she not gone running off full of suspicion.

His eyes held a rare warm look in their cool depths. As Kate met his gaze, her heart beat faster. When the tension became too strong, she looked down at her hands. "I...got breakfast. Thanks."

"And my message?"

Kate thought back over her conversation with the maid. "To relax? Yes."

"Why didn't you, then?"

Kate fiddled with the sandwich wrapping as she tried to think of an answer that would pass for the truth.

"Kate?" Max touched her shoulder.

Startled by the contact, Kate involuntarily looked at him.

"Why didn't you wait for me in the room? Or leave a message?"

"I..."

The warmth flickered out of his eyes. "You thought I was trying to scoop you, right?"

Yes, right. "Well, what was I supposed to think?" Guilt made her snap at him.

His mouth stretched in a cynical smile. "My dear, if I'd truly wanted to do you out of your exclusive photo, I could've done so on any one of a number of occasions in the past twenty-four hours. Surely you realize that."

"I realize nothing of the sort." But the longer she knew Max, the more she suspected that what he said was no boast.

"That sounds like a challenge." He shook his head. "But I won't accept challenges from you."

"Why not?" She hadn't thought of challenging him. Just getting the stupid picture was proving challenge enough. She didn't need Max complicating matters.

"Kate." He drew her name out in warning.

She didn't heed it. "Because you think scooping me wouldn't be very hard, is that it?"

He regarded her with a patronizing expression that made her blood boil. "You don't really want me to answer, do you?"

So Maxwell Hunter's ego was proving to be as great as his fame.

He thought it would be a simple matter to catch Fiona with Damian.

Kate would dearly love to prove him wrong. And she would, too, but she wouldn't be so stupid as to challenge him outright. Let him think she was backing off.

She forced a smile. "Perhaps you're right," she said. "You *are* proving to be a distraction."

She could see that this pleased him. *Men*, she thought, mentally rolling her eyes. "I would've *loved* to have spent a leisurely morning in an expensive Roman hotel, but not if it meant that I'd blow this opportunity."

"You've got me as backup."

As if that were reassuring. Kate tapped the two cameras and the lens that hung from his neck. "And what happens if you take a shot of Fiona while you're backing me up?"

"That may happen," Max conceded.

Alarm spritzed through her at his casual tone. "Let me be blunt," she said with the intensity of one heading off disaster. "In this business, exclusivity equals big bucks. If we both have pictures, the value drops. And if you get one and I don't, I'm in deep trouble." Her voice ended with a betraying quiver in spite of her best efforts.

She hated like everything to have to admit her vulnerability to Max, but she wanted him to understand.

He dropped his casual attitude at once. "Oh, Kate," he murmured. "Damn, I'm sorry." And, to her surprise, he closed his hands over hers. "I give you my word that you won't take a financial hit because of me."

And Kate believed him. Why, she couldn't say. She'd been lied to by the best of them—and the worst of them, too. It was a given in her field. Perhaps she was convinced by his intensity and the way he met her gaze straight on. Maybe it was the warmth of his hands on hers.

However... "Just let me do my job. I don't need any favors."

Shaking his head slowly, Max agreed, "No favors."

His hands, strong, confident and beautifully shaped, still covered hers. As Kate stared into his eyes, trying to read them, her anxiety seeped away. In its place grew an awareness of Max, the man, not the photographer. The afternoon breeze tickled the olive leaves and sent a constantly moving kaleidoscope of sunlight and shadow across his face. The face that was just inches away from hers.

Noises from the movie set receded to a distant buzz.

"Do you trust me now, Kate?" Max's voice mesmerized her.

She nodded dumbly.

"Good," he whispered.

Kate didn't move. She couldn't.

But Max could and did. Slowly, so that at first Kate wasn't aware of it, he angled his head downward. His gaze fastened on her mouth.

He was going to *kiss* her, Kate realized with surprise. Not that she didn't want him to, she was just amazed that it would occur to him.

Her eyes drifted shut in anticipation. She held her breath. Parted her lips. Time stopped.

Max's lips met hers in a delicate fusing that held a rich, sensual promise—a promise Kate wanted him to keep.

Max was a man who had lived and experienced life fully. He controlled life; he didn't allow life to control him. And he took control now.

His hands cupped her head as he deepened the kiss and Kate surrendered to his strength....

"Contact my agent immediately!"

Kate flinched, her eyes flying open in time to catch the pained expression on Max's face.

"Fiona!" Kate drew back.

"I don't care what time it is in Los Angeles!" The actress's voice ripped through the muted sounds of the movie set. "Call him *now*!"

"Yes, it appears our quarry has arrived," Max said, dropping a light kiss on Kate's forehead before straightening. Not at all satisfactory, but the moment was spoiled anyway.

With shaking fingers, she tucked a stray hair behind her ear and shifted away from Max.

Fiona was in fine form. Even better, she looked to be having a tantrum. Her beautiful face set in grim lines, Fiona strode toward her trailer, a group of worried-looking people jogging behind her.

She tossed her mane of hair theatrically. "Tell him I refuse to go!"

Go where? Kate wondered. Fiona's words carried clearly, which meant that any camera noises would be audible, as well.

Babble broke out among Fiona's followers as they apparently tried to convince her to go wherever it was they wanted her to go.

Kate rested the heavy telephoto lens on her knees and waited for Fiona to open her mouth. If Fiona were shouting, she wouldn't hear Kate's camera motor.

Beside her, Max maneuvered quietly. Darting a glance sideways, Kate noticed that he'd positioned a camera, but not one with a telephoto lens.

She wrestled with her conscience before finally whispering, "You should change lenses."

"This is all I've got with me," he whispered back without a trace of concern.

Kate opened her mouth to tell him that in this business, a telephoto lens was essential, then changed her mind. There was nothing she could do about Max's equipment, and besides, she didn't want to chance their whispers carrying on the wind.

Putting her camera to her eye, she waited.

"It's out of the question!" Fiona shouted and Kate popped off a shot.

Fiona angry. That could come in handy.

"I don't see Damian," Max murmured. "He was also on call this afternoon."

The scene through her viewfinder darkened and Kate had to adjust her exposure. Glancing skyward, she sighed. "If they're shooting any exteriors, they'll have to hurry."

Clouds scattered the sky like cotton balls on a makeup table.

"A delay could be good," Max pointed out. "Maybe Damian will keep her company."

"Mmm." Kate squinted through her viewfinder. "Fiona isn't in a very loving mood."

"To-ny..." Fiona yanked open her trailer door. "Tell him I need to be *seen*. I can't be *seen* in Texas..."

That was the last Kate heard as Fiona and her entourage disappeared into the dressing trailer.

"Texas?" Kate spoke aloud, momentarily forgetting about Max. "Why would they want Fiona to go to Texas?"

"To finish filming?"

"Don't be absurd." Kate dismissed Max's suggestion.

"I'm never absurd."

The tone of his statement caught Kate's attention. "You know something, don't you?"

He smiled his infuriating smile. "I know that Texas is trying to attract the film industry. They offer spectacular scenery and subsidized rates."

It made sense.

"C'mon." Kate crouched and crept forward.

"Where are we going?" Max asked from close behind her.

She held a finger to her lips. "To listen."

They approached Fiona's trailer from the back, squatting under the window. Kate pressed her ear against the side.

It wasn't necessary. Fiona was complaining long and loud. "But, Tony, I can't get back into the Hollywood scene if I'm stuck in *Texas*." She made it sound like a provincial backwater. "*Why* doesn't Winthrop understand?"

"Darling, the movie is over budget," answered a male voice Kate assumed was Tony's. "Production costs will be lower in Texas. *That's* what your husband understands."

So Max was right. As usual.

Kate had heard enough. Knowing Fiona as she did, she knew the actress would pout and cause a further delay. She also knew that Fiona was likely to rebel sooner or later. Kate hoped it would be sooner.

Signaling Max, she crept back to her cover of olive trees. "I suppose now you'll gloat," she said as soon as they were out of earshot.

"I'm entitled."

"So gloat." Kate sighed and leaned against a tree. Off in the distance, the extras huddled in clusters. The clouds knit together and the air cooled. Kate smelled rain.

"Are you ready to go back to the hotel?" Max asked.

Since she'd packed everything she owned this morning, Max probably guessed that she had no intention of returning to the Principe. He was just going to make her say it out loud.

Well, she wouldn't. "You can go on ahead. I'm staying here."

"Kate—" Max started to say something, then obviously changed his mind. "Look." He pointed to the stone farmhouse. "They're dismissing the extras. It'll probably rain."

Kate unzipped her duffel and withdrew her rain poncho. "They're not dismissing them—they're filming."

"It's still going to rain. And what do you think you're going to accomplish out here? Come back with me."

Kate shook her head.

"I'll order a fabulous dinner," he promised. "The Principe's restaurant is world-class."

"I'm sure it is."

"But?"

Deliberately, Kate crawled into her poncho. "My job is to take pictures of Fiona and Damian, not dine in expensive Roman restaurants or stay in expensive Roman hotels and stick somebody else with the bill." There. She'd said it. She'd been longing to say it. And until she'd said it, she hadn't realized how *much* she resented Max's seemingly unlimited funds.

The air around her cooled, as much from Max's manner as from the weather.

"Did it occur to you that I might have chosen the Principe for a reason?" He clipped off his words, each one sharply distinct.

CHAPTER FIVE

MAX'S parting comment made Kate very nervous. So nervous that she forgot to cover her sandwiches.

Max was completely sure of himself. She watched him tramp through the trees and walk right out into the open as if he were the official set photographer. Nobody bothered him. No one questioned him. No one would *dare* question him.

That would change, she consoled herself. Just let Max catch a few stars when they thought they were in private, and doors now open to him would close right in his face. Then he'd see what it was like to be scorned and avoided.

Shrouded from head to toe in black plastic, Kate boldly carried the sodden remains of her lunch to the catering truck and dumped the entire mess into a trash barrel. If Max could do it, so could she. Besides, nobody would recognize her anyway.

Which was good, because not long after Max left, Fiona, in costume, emerged from her trailer. The rain had stopped for the moment and it appeared that filming would resume.

With Max's words ringing in her ears, Kate became more daring and wandered close enough to the action to mingle with the extras who waited out of camera range.

Fiona stood in the doorway of the farmhouse and overacted an impassioned plea to the angry villagers.

After the scene had been repeated and filmed from different camera angles, Fiona, surrounded by her entourage, swept past the extras.

"Don't worry, babe, we'll get the publicist working on it," Kate heard and guessed that Fiona was still angry that she wouldn't be returning to Hollywood.

Maintaining a discreet distance, Kate followed the actress back to her dressing trailer and crouched under the same window as she and Max had earlier.

Her patience was rewarded when she heard Fiona mention Damian and dinner in the same breath. She just didn't mention where.

Sighing, Kate resigned herself to another evening of chase. She only hoped Fiona was hungry.

But Fiona went shopping.

It fit right in. She was angry with her husband and so she punished him by spending his money. And she was spending it at the exclusive Sfara Boutique near the Spanish Steps.

Kate drove her car as close as she could, then parked it. It was pointless to try to sneak past the doorman, so she and Fiona's driver waited in the dripping dusk. Kate didn't like waiting, but usually resigned herself to it. Leaning with her back against the car door, she pulled a paperback novel out of her bag and tried to read.

Unfortunately, thoughts of Max intruded.

She'd probably seen the last of him, since she had no intention of returning to the Principe and every intention of getting the picture she wanted tonight.

All the elements were in place: Fiona angry at her husband, that same husband back in the United States, Fiona's latest *amore* meeting her for dinner... With any luck at all, Kate should get some fabulous shots of Damian comforting Fiona while Max enjoyed his splendid dinner at the Principe. And about the time he was trading war stories with Giordano, Kate would be at the airport with a ticket on the next flight to the States.

She smiled in satisfaction. Max might be an eminent photojournalist, but he still had a lot to learn about celebrity photography. And discovering that he should have stayed with her was the best way for him to learn.

On the other hand, he had a way of making his own opportunities and she shouldn't underestimate him.

Giving up and putting away her book, Kate scanned the entrance to Sfara's half-expecting to find Max waltzing out with Fiona on his arm. However, Fiona, now attired in a dinner dress, waltzed out alone.

A dinner dress. Kate was cheered. This was no quiet evening on the town—or a dinner in her hotel room, which had been a distinct possibility.

Fiona headed straight for Raphael's, a Roman hot spot. Across the street, there was an outdoor café that would be a perfect stakeout spot for Kate. She parked her car some distance away. Hiding her camera under the plastic poncho, she picked a table where she could see into Raphael's restaurant area, and ordered cappuccino.

Three expensive cappuccinos later, Damian finally arrived.

Too bad he wasn't alone.

Peering through her telephoto lens, Kate saw Fiona and Damian take their places at opposite ends of a long table filled with people. Great. A party of some sort and the two lovebirds were well chaperoned.

Still Kate waited and watched. When it began to drizzle again, the waiter shooed her away before turning off the lights and pulling the wrought-iron furniture inside.

Sighing, she began walking a circuit that took her past Raphael's frequently enough that the doorman eyed her suspiciously.

And Max thought her job was fun?

Retrieving her car, Kate risked parking it on the street and stayed there undisturbed until the party ended.

It was with a sense of futility that she watched Fiona climb into one car and Damian get into another, then head in opposite directions. Kate mentally flipped a coin and followed Fiona, hoping that Fiona and Damian were being extremely discreet and would meet later.

By the time Fiona's car pulled in front of the imposing-looking Hotel da Vinci, Kate felt like crying. She was wet, hungry, tired, frustrated and had to go to the bathroom.

And the Hotel da Vinci was right across the street from the Principe.

Max must have known. He probably even knew about the dinner party at Raphael's. He was probably laughing at her right now.

Nevertheless, Kate parked her car and waited. Sooner or later, either Damian would come to Fiona, or Fiona would go to Damian. And Kate would follow and record the event for posterity—or the week *World Eye* was on the newsstands.

Kate hadn't even realized she'd been asleep when a tapping on her car window woke her up. Startled, she sat up quickly, then got another jolt before she recognized the man peering inside her car.

Max.

Of course.

Kate lowered her window and gazed at him defiantly.

"Hello, Kate."

"Hello, Max."

He'd changed from the khaki cotton slacks he'd worn earlier. His shirt was crisp and white. Kate was limp and black.

"Giordano will be extremely distressed to discover that you prefer sleeping in your car to staying in his hotel."

"I'm working, Max."

"Yes, I saw," he replied in an amused drawl.

Kate was glad of the darkness as she felt her cheeks heat. What time was it anyway?

"Are you cold?"

"Mostly damp," she admitted.

"Would you like to come upstairs now?"

"No."

Max straightened. "I knew you'd say that."

Kate deliberately trained her gaze on the entrance to the Hotel da Vinci. So the evening had been a complete waste up until now. Sometimes that happened.

"Hungry?"

Admit hunger after all the sandwich cracks this afternoon? "Not really."

Kate heard a metallic scrape. The aroma of tomatoes and spices filled her little car. "What do I smell?" She turned her head and stared directly into a bowl of minestrone. Steaming minestrone.

Max's face appeared next to the bowl. He held up a spoon. "Dinner?"

"Thanks." Kate allowed a reluctant grin and accepted the plate and spoon.

Moments later, Max joined her in the car. "It wasn't the dinner I had planned for you, but I thought you might enjoy it."

"Wonderful," Kate managed between mouthfuls. She felt warm inside and suspected it was as much from Max's thoughtfulness as from the soup. She hadn't really wanted them to part in anger.

"Did you know Fiona was staying at the da Vinci?"

"Signor Giordano told me when we arrived."

"Why didn't you tell me?"

"I'd planned to," he said quietly. "This morning."

"Oh." Kate chased a macaroni shell with her spoon. Much as she'd wanted to fault him, she couldn't.

The steam from the soup and the warmth of another person fogged the windows of the car. She rubbed a spot on the windshield so she could keep an eye on the da Vinci's entrance.

Max turned his back to the entrance and watched her eat. Kate was too hungry to worry about how she must look slurping soup in a car.

When she'd finished, Max handed her a cloth napkin. "No luck this evening?"

Kate shook her head. "I wouldn't be sitting here if I had."

"Planning to stay out here all night?"

"Or until Damian arrives."

"I thought you wanted pictures of them together." Max covered her empty bowl with the metal dome. "Damian entering a five-star hotel is hardly newsworthy."

"You're right." Kate squinted against the headlights from an approaching vehicle. "Hey!" She thrust her dishes at Max. "The car's stopping."

"It could be anyone."

But Kate had already positioned her camera. "I have a feeling . . ."

The doorman ran down the steps and opened the car door. Damian Carney emerged.

"Bingo!" Kate shot pictures until he disappeared inside.

"Congratulations" was Max's unimpressed comment. "Now will you come up to the room?"

"Why?" she asked in surprise. "I realize I don't have much, but now that I know he's in there, I'll wait here, then hang around the lobby in the morning."

"No, you won't," Max announced. "You're an extremely stubborn woman, but it's time to give in and come inside."

If he'd used any other tone of voice... "No."

"Kate..." Max's mouth worked. Swiveling around, he looked up at the da Vinci. "Now. Come with me now."

"I will not!"

Max alarmed her the way he stormed out of the car and jerked open her door.

"Get out of the car, or I'll drag you out."

He would, too. She could see by the set of his jaw. He'd probably enjoy it if she struggled. "Force, Mr. Hunter?"

"Force, Miss Brandon." His voice was unapologetically firm.

Kate took her time emerging from the car.

"Get your camera," Max ordered and grabbed her wrist.

Kate barely had enough time to sling her bag over her shoulder before she was hauled along the sidewalk and hustled into the Principe.

"Do you always use force to get your way?" she asked in her sweetest voice.

"I generally don't have to." He gave her a wintry glance and jabbed the elevator button.

"Does the thought of me sleeping in the car make you feel guilty for laying out a lot of lira for that room?"

He didn't answer, but Kate knew she was right. How could he possibly justify the expense of that room for just one person?

He took her arm as soon as the elevator doors opened. He didn't hurt her, but she was in no doubt of his irritation.

Using the ornate old-fashioned key to unlock the suite, he stood aside. "After you," he said with an exaggerated bow.

The lights were off and the curtains open. Max's camera was set on a tripod in front of the window. As Kate stared, she heard the click and whir of the timer triggering the camera.

"What's all this?"

In answer, he pointed.

Kate dropped her bag on the sofa and walked over to the window. Even this late, a few room lights from the da Vinci glowed. Max's camera was focused on the one directly across. Already suspecting what she'd see, Kate bent and looked through the viewfinder.

There, talking on the telephone and gesturing wildly, was Fiona Ferguson.

Without looking at Max, Kate retrieved her camera bag and withdrew her camera.

"Aren't you going to say anything?" he asked finally.

"My telephoto lens is better than yours."

"Agreed. Anything else?"

Kate looked away from the window long enough to glare at him. "Why didn't you just tell me?"

"I tried. You weren't listening."

"I did not hear the words 'our room looks directly into Fiona's'."

"No." Max crossed his arms and wandered closer. "Of course, that's the reason I rented this room. I resented the way you thought I was living it up on an expense account."

Kate moved a chair next to the window and propped her camera on it. "How could you have known which room Fiona was staying in? We arrived in the middle of the night and she was just a few hours ahead of us."

"I didn't, but the suites are on the top floors in both hotels. It was a calculated guess."

And a good one. Kate geared herself up to admit it and found it surprisingly hard to do so. She knew she was being childish, but darn it, Max had bested her in each encounter they'd had. *She* was supposed to be the expert.

"Thanks." Very inadequate. Even a bit surly, but it was all she could manage right now.

His camera clicked again, providing a distraction. "Are you going to take the timer off?"

"Only if things heat up."

Kate nodded stiffly and peered through her own camera. "Fiona's probably complaining to her husband or her agent."

"Find Damian yet?"

Shifting slightly, Kate located him on a couch in the living area. "He's watching a movie."

Max hunched down next to her on the floor. "Can you tell which one?"

"For what this lens cost, I'd better be able to," Kate said as she refocused her camera.

"Well?"

Clearing her throat, she looked at Max. "I'm not familiar with that...genre."

"Oh." He raised his eyebrows.

"Get off the phone, Fiona," Kate muttered. "Don't you know better than to make transatlantic calls from your hotel room?"

Max reached for the sofa pillows and handed her one. "You don't know for a fact that she's called the States."

Kate knelt on the pillow. "Yes, I do. I know Fiona. I know how her mind works. What'll happen next is that she'll either turn to Damian for comfort—which is what I want—or she'll continue her tantrum and he'll leave."

"Which you don't want."

"No." Since Fiona was still talking, Kate panned the area. "The curtains are drawn in the bedroom."

"Would *World Eye* print pictures of them in the bedroom?"

"Glen *lives* for bedroom shots. That's the sort of man he is," Kate informed him as she zoomed in on Fiona again. "He keeps telling me how scandal and embarrassment is great for circulation."

"The tabloid business really is no holds barred." Max sounded impressed. And dangerous. "This is great. Just what I've been looking for. Someone who's got the guts to publish my pictures."

He could be the kind of photographer who got out of control. "Now hold on," Kate cautioned him. "There are laws, you know."

"And I want to walk in the shadow right next to the legal line." Max grinned and settled back against the couch.

Kate raised her head. "Which side of the line?"

"The side with the best pictures," he retorted.

Kate guessed that Max was familiar with the gray areas of life. She leveled a look at him. "Hope you've got a good lawyer on retainer."

Max gave an unconcerned laugh.

"I'm serious," Kate insisted. "And don't think *World Eye* will pick up your legal tab if you're convicted of harassment."

"You've got to take risks, Kate. You know that." And she could tell Max was looking forward to those risks.

"Celebrities are funny," she said. "When they're nobodies, they hire publicists to court the media. They send out press releases, create photo ops. Invite us to parties. And then, they hit it big and all at once the press is scum. They whine about their privacy—until they've got a new movie to plug."

"Scum?" Max raised an eyebrow in disbelief.

"And that's probably the nicest name I've been called." She peered through her telephoto lens. Fiona was still talking. Damian was still watching the smutty movie. "Think you can handle the change from respected journalist to scum?"

Max didn't respond.

"Nothing to say?"

"I'm thinking."

"Think fast. Fiona's off the phone."

Instantly, Max was on his feet at his own camera. "I'm pulling wide, so you can close in without worrying about losing them."

"Okay." She held her breath. "Rats. She joined him on the sofa and their faces don't show. They could be anybody." Nevertheless, Kate snapped a few frames.

"Patience."

She needed it. Occasionally, Fiona lifted her head, obviously recounting her conversation on the telephone. Damian just as obviously wanted to watch his movie.

Eventually, Fiona flounced off to the bedroom. Still Kate watched, hoping that Fiona would reappear in sexy lingerie and try to compete with the movie.

She didn't. And twenty minutes later, Damian turned off the light and followed her.

Kate sighed and lowered her camera.

"I'll reload and set the timer in case there's any nocturnal activity," Max offered.

"Thanks." Kate was suddenly very tired. Moving off the pillow, she slumped against the sofa and closed her eyes.

The evening that had started out so promising was so disappointing. Thanks to Max, they had the perfect location and Damian was actually with Fiona. In the same hotel room. Alone. How could Kate not get her picture?

Oh, she had pictures, but nothing worth printing. Later, perhaps, if—when—she broke the Damian/Fiona affair, the pictures would work, but only as follow-up fillers.

"All set up." Max dropped to the floor beside her. "Now what?"

"Now we wait."

"How long?"

"As long as it takes."

"Kate." She heard an exasperated sigh. "They've gone to bed. Shouldn't we get some sleep, too?"

"I hardly think they're sleeping," she mumbled.

"With the curtains drawn, it doesn't matter what they're doing."

"Actually, I'm waiting to see if they throw open the curtains and step out onto the balcony to cool off and take in the view." That's what Kate would do. How could Fiona and Damian resist all of Rome spread out at their feet and a canopy of stars overhead?

"You're going to sit here all night?"

"Maybe." Without lifting her head, she turned to look at him. "Exciting, isn't it?"

He regarded her for a moment. "It could be."

A sarcastic response popped into Kate's mind, but she didn't utter it. For once, her cynical nature was overpowered by something softer and more feminine.

Max's face was half in shadow, half bathed in the reflected glow of floodlights on ancient Roman buildings.

Life could be exciting.

You've got to take risks, Kate. You know that. Max had been speaking of photography, but he could have been referring to her life.

She'd played it too safe, too alone. For ten days, she'd watched and waited for her chance at Fiona. Max wouldn't have waited. *Hadn't* waited. Max made things happen.

Except now. Now he waited, studying her with a photographer's eye.

And Kate was tired of waiting. She'd spent her adult life waiting for things to happen to other people. It was time for life to happen to her.

After so many years of passing her by, life was going to need a little nudge. Kate's fingers trembled slightly as she loosened them from where they'd been clasped around her knees. Shifting away from the sofa, she straightened until she could look down at Max.

The time he'd spent outside in the damp with her had made his hair curl slightly and a section had fallen over his forehead. Kate smoothed it back to the side.

She heard him inhale, not a gasp, but enough to know that her touch had affected him. The knowledge provided the encouragement she desperately needed.

With both hands, she cupped his face, feeling the muscles in his jaw tense, feeling the roughness of his day-old beard.

He smiled.

And she lowered her mouth to his.

CHAPTER SIX

KATE had never kissed a man before.

Been kissed *by*, but had never made the first move. It was risky to make the first move.

But now she discovered it was also empowering. She set the pace. She decided how deep the kiss would be. And she'd decide when it was over. She was in control.

For about three seconds.

That was how long it took for her to stop *thinking* about what she was doing and to start *feeling*. And what she was feeling was passion, a passion so deep and unexpected that it overwhelmed all conscious thought.

Their brief kiss this afternoon had been full of promise.

This was promise fulfilled.

Before she closed her eyes, Kate lost herself in the roughness of Max's beard, the scent of the Principe's herbal soap and the shadowed light from the open window.

Max's lips were warmly responsive beneath hers. He matched her movements, allowing her control of this kiss.

For about three seconds.

With a soft groan as if he couldn't help himself, his hands slipped under her T-shirt and splayed across her back.

Kate trembled as raw desire unfurled within her. Nothing she'd ever felt with anyone else had prepared her for the strength of it. From deep inside it flared, and with each beat, her heart pulsed it throughout her body.

She felt Max bury his hand beneath the hair at her nape before his arms tightened around her, pulling her with him as he stretched onto the carpet.

And still she wasn't close enough. She'd never be close enough. Breaking the kiss to scoot upward, her foot caught the leg of Max's tripod. She froze, then gasped as the camera and tripod came crashing down.

She braced herself, hoping the camera would land on her instead of the marble floor next to the window. But rather than the sickening smack of metal, she heard a soft grunt.

Arms outstretched, Max had caught the tip of the tripod, breaking its fall. Kate didn't move as he lowered it gently to one side.

"I'm so sorry!" Shaking with reaction to the near disaster as much as the kiss, she got to her knees.

"No harm done." Max ran his fingers through his hair and levered himself to his feet, reaching to help her up. "Shall we use this opportunity to adjourn to a more comfortable…?" He trailed off as Kate shook her head.

Her nerve was gone. Her control was gone.

"Too fast?" he asked, trying to see her face when she looked down.

"Too much." She needed time to absorb the changes she'd discovered in herself this evening.

Max drew her gently to him. "I know," he whispered, his hand caressing her. "I feel it, too."

"You do?" She looked up, trying to read his expression.

He nodded, but Kate didn't believe him. He couldn't possibly feel the desperate hunger for her touch that she felt for his. Not after such a short time.

Kate drew a shuddering breath, then another to calm her racing pulse. She'd been alone for too long, that was all. She apparently needed physical contact with another being more than she realized.

Maybe she should get a pet.

Max held her until she pushed gently away. He let her go without protest and busied himself righting the camera tripod, allowing her to compose herself.

Kate bent and picked up the pillows, hugging one to her as she sank onto the sofa. Max was being awfully decent after she'd...she'd...just what *had* she intended?

Two days ago, Maxwell Hunter had only been a name. Now, she couldn't imagine ever not knowing him. Since meeting Max, everything had changed. *She'd* changed.

Max peered through the viewfinder and set up his shot. Then he adjusted the timer and turned to her with a smile. "No damage done."

At least to the camera. Kate gripped the pillow. She saw Max's gaze flick over her and she tried to smile as if all were well. One side of her mouth didn't quite catch up to the other.

"Coffee?"

"It's kind of late for coffee." She should have said yes. It would have given her something to do with her hands.

"I suppose so." Max glanced out the window. "No sign of the lovebirds."

He joined her on the sofa and threw an arm around her shoulders. She flinched and hated herself for it.

"Kate."

She looked away.

He nudged her chin until she faced him. "I enjoyed kissing you. Very much."

Her face grew hot and she was glad the room was dark.

"And I enjoyed it for what it was, not what it might have been or where it might have led. Although..."

"What?" she prompted.

"I do wish the tripod hadn't fallen."

He sounded so wistful that Kate surprised herself by laughing and the tension was broken.

Rather than joining her in laughter, Max watched her, an amused smile on his face.

"What is it?" Kate asked, wondering about that smile.

"You have a nice laugh—low and throaty. Sexy."

Kate blinked, then lowered her gaze.

She felt his hand shift from the back of the sofa to her shoulder. His thumb slowly moved in gentle circles. "This is the first time I've heard you laugh."

Kate shrugged. "I don't find much to laugh about."

"Such a serious person for such an unserious business."

"To you, maybe. I take it very seriously."

Max gestured to the window. "What's serious about trying to catch a B-grade actress with her equally B-grade lover?"

Kate shot him a look. "We don't know that he's a B-grade lover."

"Kate!" Drawing back, Max regarded her in mock surprise. "You made a joke."

"A very small one."

Chuckling, he pulled her close. "How *did* you get into stealth photography?"

Kate laughed again. It was easier this time. "I was out photographing people for my stock files. I went to the zoo and bingo, there was Marsha Masterson with her daughter and nanny."

Max raised his eyebrows. "Was this before or after she made *Singapore Fling*?"

"I think during," Kate answered. "Anyway, I didn't even recognize her at first. She had on sunglasses, shorts and a cap. She could have been anybody. But I thought the little girl was cute and had taken several photographs of her before this woman hustled her off. I followed them to apologize and explain that I was harmless—and to get a model release—and that's when I recognized one of the women was Marsha Masterson.''

"I'm surprised you got that far," Max commented. "Where was her bodyguard?"

"I never saw a bodyguard." Kate had been incredibly lucky that day. Sometimes it happened that way, but most of the time it didn't. "I popped off some shots. When I developed the film, I saw that I'd actually caught her with her daughter in an earlier frame."

"I've had luck like that. Both good and bad." Max had a faraway look in his eyes. "So then what? How did you know what to do with the picture?"

Kate shook her head. "I didn't. I called my stock agency and they handled the sale for me. To *World Eye*, actually."

"Minus a hefty fee, I'll bet."

"But still . . ." Kate remembered staring at the check, unable to believe it. It was ten times what she'd been paid for her feature illustrations. "Pictures of Marsha's daughter are so rare that I lived for two months off the sale of that one picture."

Max whistled.

"*You* might have lived for a week."

"Probably," he agreed without rancor. "But it would've been a heck of a week."

This time, Kate's laughter was full and uninhibited. "I guess that's the basic difference between us," she said when she could. "I've been too careful."

"Not really. Supporting yourself by free-lancing takes guts. You've got to make the most of what security you can."

"I suppose." Kate stared out the window at Fiona's darkened suite. How secure was trailing a has-been actress to Rome?

Max must have been thinking along the same lines. "Why Fiona?"

"Her hair. It was easier to find her in the crowds." Kate grinned. "I started hanging out at the zoo until I got smart and began to read the society columns and go where the action was. There are a lot more stars at movie premieres than at the zoo. Fiona figured that out, too."

It was quiet and dark and Max was a willing listener. Kate found herself telling him how Fiona had singled her out.

Fiona was ambitious and needed publicity. Together she and Kate stalked celebrities. Fiona would approach them, pose as if she belonged with them, and Kate would snap a picture. Fiona would even write her own copy. By then, Glen noticed what celebrity photos did for *World Eye*'s sales and her collaboration with Fiona was a profitable one. Fiona's picture appeared in *World Eye* enough times to attract the attention of a better agent, who got her some small parts, and she was on her way.

Kate went with her. As Fiona became more well-known, her pictures increased in value.

"So what happened to your partnership?" Max asked when Kate fell silent.

Should she tell him the true reason she was so determined to catch Fiona with Damian? Maybe if Max realized it was more than just the money…although that was a large part of it. "We had a falling out," she said, trying to gauge his reaction.

"Over one of your photographs?"

"No," Kate answered him slowly, "over my brother."

Max raised his brows. "Are you planning to elaborate or leave me dangling?"

Smiling ruefully, Kate toyed with the fringe on one of the sofa pillows. "I grew up the fourth of five kids in a Midwest farm family. As long as I can remember, I wanted off that farm. I didn't fit in." She shrugged. "My family was hardworking and loving, but they didn't understand why I wanted to see the world and I couldn't understand how they could be satisfied staying in one place all their lives when a whole world was waiting to be explored."

"How old were you when you left?"

"Eighteen, right out of high school."

"Did you run away?"

"Oh, no." Kate looked up from the pillow. "My parents were actually relieved, and even though money was tight, they insisted on helping me get started." She grinned. "It felt great to be able to pay them back."

"Tell me," Max said, stretching his legs out in front of him, "was the world everything you thought it would be?"

Kate shrugged. "I had to adjust my expectations, naturally, but I've never regretted leaving."

"So where does your brother fit in?"

A year had passed, but Kate still found the memories painful. "Jonathan is my little brother and I'm closer to him than any of the others. I'd write him about my exciting and glamorous life in the big city." She made a face and Max chuckled with understanding.

"I encouraged him to come and visit me—none of my family ever had. You see, he'd gone to junior college and was going to get married to a local girl. Anyway, I thought he was too young to settle down. I guess I wanted to show him that there was a different world. My world." Kate's mouth tightened. "Unfortunately, my world included Fiona."

"He fell for her, didn't he?"

Kate nodded. "And she let him."

"Kate," he said in his deep voice, "you can't stop someone from falling in love with you."

"Well, you don't have to encourage it," she insisted stubbornly. "Jonathan was so green and Fiona was older and much, *much*," she added self-righteously, "more experienced."

"Did you ever consider that she might have loved him?"

"Oh, please." Kate got up and headed to the small bar. "Would you like anything?"

Max looked over the back of the sofa. "Are there any good sodas in the fridge?"

Kate bent to peer into the tiny cooler and picked a bottle. Pouring two glasses, she felt able to continue her story. "You see, Fiona's career stalled after she got involved with one of her leading men. It seems her lover was married to the producer's daughter."

"Ouch."

"Right. She was hanging out with me because by this time, Glen was encouraging racy photos and she wanted to jump-start her career by pandering to that element. The other publications I free-lanced for weren't all that interested in her. So, when I was on assignment for one of them, Fiona offered to show *Johnny*," Kate imitated Fiona's breathy voice, "around."

Groaning as she remembered how quickly Fiona had charmed her brother, Kate handed Max a glass and sat next to him. "I should have seen it coming. She's an *actress*. She *acted* as though she was in love with him—until he ran out of money."

Max sipped his soda. "Don't you think Jonathan should share some of the responsibility? Sounds as though you're being an overprotective sister."

"But it's my fault!" Kate slammed her glass down on the marble table. "If I hadn't invited him to come to Los Angeles, he wouldn't have met Fiona. He even broke his engagement."

"If he was willing to break an engagement that quickly, then he wasn't ready to get married. I'm sorry, Kate," Max said, shaking his head, "but I still don't think you should accept all the blame."

"But I do. You weren't there. You didn't see him. He was devastated. She ruined his life." And in an ugly scene, Kate had told Fiona as much. Kate also refused to give the redhead any more publicity.

Fiona retaliated by selling exclusive rights of her wedding to Winthrop to *Global Celebrity*, *World Eye*'s competitor. Glen had been livid.

"Aren't you being overdramatic?" Max asked. "Jonathan is probably over it by now."

"No." Kate stared out the window to the da Vinci. "Midwestern farmers don't have a lot of money. He left here with nothing. He's never married and works as a hired hand for my sister and her husband on their farm." Kate's voice cracked as she remembered her brother and his plans for his own home.

"It does seem to be a harsh lesson." Max thought a moment. "Does your family blame you?"

"I told Mom what happened and no one ever mentioned it again. They don't have to." Kate continued to stare out the window. No activity from the da Vinci. "I'm going to make it up to him." She turned back to Max. "I'm going to catch her cheating on her husband and show Jonathan that she isn't worth his love. And I'm going to pay him back with the money I earn from the picture."

Max smiled widely. "Poetic justice. I like it."

"Exactly." Kate looked at Max. "That's why *I* want the picture. I want to take the picture that breaks this story and I want her to know it."

Max brought a finger to his mouth as he thought. "How long have we been sitting here?"

Kate shook her head.

"Long enough, I think." He got to his feet and strode over to the telephone table. Picking up the receiver, he winked at Kate. "Let's make something happen."

As Kate listened, Max had the hotel operator put him through to the da Vinci where he ordered breakfast for two served on the terrace. "With any luck, they'll still be in their nightclothes. And we'll nab them."

"They're not going to fall for that," Kate said, impressed in spite of herself.

"Sure they will." Max tugged her to her feet. "They'll think it's compliments of the hotel."

"Who's paying for it?"

Max grinned, flashing white teeth in an increasingly dark beard. "They are."

"That's... that's..." Kate knew she should protest, but... "That's brilliant."

"I know." Max laughed and drew her into his arms. "Now, kiss me good-night and let's get some sleep."

It was the most natural thing in the world for Kate to raise her mouth to his. She was prepared for the desire this time, but not for the way Max's mouth moved over hers with an ease that spoke of much practice. All Kate had going for her was eagerness and a few second thoughts. Just as the first doubts crept into her response, Max broke the kiss, twirled her around and gave her a gentle push toward her bedroom.

"Go. Now. While you can."

Surprised, Kate looked back over her shoulder.

The look on Max's face sent her scurrying to the bedroom, her heart pounding, her mouth smiling.

The next morning, Kate shot up in bed, instantly awake and feeling an impending sense of doom. It was so strong that she ran from the room clad only in her T-shirt.

Immediately, she noticed that Max's camera wasn't sitting on its tripod in front of the window.

As she stood blinking and gazing around the room, she saw her reflection in the bar mirror. Rumpled was too kind a word.

Her shirt barely stretched to the tops of her thighs, and her hair... Running her fingers through it, Kate crept across the living area to Max's bedroom.

Without bothering to knock, she pushed open the door, knowing she'd find the room empty.

And it was.

Max had packed up all his gear and left with only the scent of his shaving soap lingering in the air.

Kate ran back to the telephone table hoping for a note. Nothing.

A flash of white from the da Vinci caught her eye.

Staring through a gray Roman drizzle, Kate saw two uniformed maids open the drapes. The doors to the terrace remained closed. There was no evidence of breakfast.

Of course not. It was raining. Kate sat on the arm of the sofa and watched the maids clean Fiona's room.

What time was it? Searching for the ornate clock on the fireplace mantel, Kate saw the black, filigreed hands pointing to ten o'clock.

That couldn't be right.

Still muzzy-headed, she returned to her room for her watch. Ten o'clock.

No. It couldn't be ten o'clock. It couldn't be.

"Max!" His name was ripped from her.

There was no answer. Kate ran back to the living area and searched for a note. Max wasn't there. He would have left a note. Surely after last night he'd leave a note. Surely he would.

Max wasn't the kind of man to walk away without a goodbye. It wasn't his style. There must be some explanation.

But as Kate tore through the suite, she could find no trace of Max. Her search brought her back to the window. The maids continued to clean.

Fiona was gone.

And so was Max.

Swallowing hard, Kate wondered if she'd been betrayed. Again. Was anyone ever as stupid as she? *Why* couldn't she learn? Why did she continue to trust people time after time?

Because she'd thought *this time* was different.

Remembering how she'd practically *attacked* Max, Kate moaned and covered her face. He'd certainly read her right. She was lonely and sex-starved. Easy pickings.

Now he was gone. After she'd made her way to bed, he'd probably caught Fiona and Damian and was headed back to Glen at *World Eye* even now.

She hoped he'd paid their bill first.

But why should he? At that thought, Kate was overcome by a wave of nausea.

What if he hadn't paid the bill? There was no way she could...

And she wouldn't, not if she had to climb down the gray stone of the Principe's front facade. Gritting her teeth, Kate marched into her room and dressed. *She* wasn't about to pick up this tab. Max had checked in.

Let Max pay the bill. Kate had been the stupid victim long enough.

Splashing water on her face, she turned off the tap in time to hear the telephone ringing.

She almost didn't answer it, but the phone wouldn't stop ringing. "Hello?"

"Kate?"

It was Max. Kate didn't know how to react.

He didn't give her time to. "Wake up."

"I'm awake."

The anger in her voice must not have registered with him. "Hurry up and get to the airport. And I mean hurry. Fiona and Damian are flying out of here and I got us two tickets on their flight. You've got forty-five minutes at the most."

"But—"

"I checked us out already. *Move.*"

"Okay, I—"

"Alitalia. See you."

Kate hated rushing to the airport. Fortunately, her cabdriver enjoyed the challenge. Thrusting all her remaining lira at him, she tore into the airport and raced to the Alitalia counter to have Max paged.

He caught up with her first. "C'mon."

With Max's press pass greasing the way, they made it aboard the flight, which had been delayed.

"That's lucky," Kate commented, feeling jittery, and she hadn't even had any coffee this morning.

"Luck had nothing to do with it," Max said.

"You mean you...?"

He nodded. "I'm a heavy tipper."

Kate couldn't bear to ask how heavy.

"Sorry these are only coach," Max apologized as they struggled into their seats. "I didn't want to chance Fiona recognizing you in first class."

"Good thinking. I'll just struggle along here with the peons." Like she'd know any difference. She closed her eyes, desperate for coffee.

"We made it," Max said. "You can calm down now."

Kate swallowed.

"Did you think I'd deserted you?"

"Yes," she said, her eyes still closed.

"Damn. I figured you would."

At that, she opened her eyes.

"Giovanni called me this morning when it started to rain. Did you hear the phone?"

Kate shook her head. "You told him about the breakfast?"

"I thought about what you said last night and wanted to make sure that if something happened and the da Vinci *didn't* deliver breakfast, another one would be ordered."

"Oh."

"The rain messed us up. I packed everything but my camera and then I saw the limos. I yelled at you, but I guess you didn't wake up."

"I didn't hear a thing."

"I just grabbed my gear and followed them. I didn't know they were going to the airport. I would've called you, but I wanted to get tickets first."

She owed him. A lot. But she didn't want to think about it. "Thanks."

Once again, Max had rescued her. She would have completely missed Fiona and Damian if she'd been by herself.

Kate watched the ground recede as the plane climbed toward cruising altitude. "Max?"

"I already tried to get coffee. They're going to make us wait our turn." He sounded disgusted.

Kate smiled. "I was going to ask what would have happened if I hadn't been able to make this flight. Would you have gone on?"

"No," he answered, looking surprised that she had considered it a possibility. "Why would I?"

"To get Fiona and Damian, of course."

He shifted until he was facing her. "I don't want Fiona and Damian," he said deliberately. "I want you."

CHAPTER SEVEN

KATE was immediately and fully awake—even without coffee. She felt as though she'd left her stomach behind in Rome. All she could do was stare, openmouthed, at an increasingly amused Max. As his smile widened, Kate's heart thudded until she thought he must surely hear it.

"Too direct?"

"Uh..." Memories of the way his mouth had felt against hers triggered a replay of the moments before the tripod fell.

"I'm used to moving fast. The way I've bounced from country to country, there's never been time for slow and subtle."

Kate managed to close her mouth.

He covered one of her white-knuckled fists with his fingers. Goose bumps broke out along her arms. "This is a nine-hour flight. Plenty of time for us to trade life stories. By the time we land in New York, we'll either be sick of each other or..."

"Or?"

He grinned. "Let's see what develops."

She couldn't believe he'd said that. Rolling her eyes, Kate moved her hand out from under his. "Nothing's going to develop if you make corny photographer jokes."

"You have no sense of humor."

She adjusted the air control above her seat. "On the contrary, I have a highly refined sense of humor." It went so nicely with her highly refined sense of desire, which she was doing her best to control.

Looking at Max didn't help at all, so she looked out the window. There was nothing to distract her but clouds.

The fact was, she and Max had no future together. For a while, she'd thought a fling was a possibility, but now knew it wasn't unless she wanted to get hurt. The trouble was, she'd want more from Max than he'd be able to give her. It was best if she just kept things light between them.

Max might think he was retired, but Kate knew that he'd quickly miss the excitement of a photojournalist's life. Already, he was dabbling in *her* field, thinking it would make a good substitute for what he'd rather be doing.

No, Max wouldn't be able to stay in one place for long, and frankly, would she?

"I hope your mood improves after coffee," he said, watching two flight attendants push the serving cart down the aisle.

Privately, she doubted it. The bonus of meeting Max aside, it was time to face the fact that she'd spent two weeks and a lot of money chasing Fiona and still didn't have a picture to suit Glen or to convince her brother to forget Fiona. Of course, the trip hadn't been a total waste. She now knew for certain that Fiona was involved with Damian, and once she caught them in a compromising position, several of her other shots would work as the story ran its course.

Kate tried to see into the first-class cabin, but the flight attendants kept the curtain tightly drawn. She and Max were seated close enough to the front of the plane that she could hear laughter and snatches of conversation, but nothing she could make out. "Do you suppose all the movie bigwigs are on this flight?"

"I don't think so," Max answered. "I have the impression that our lovebirds are traveling with an entourage of underlings."

"Do you think it's worth trying to get pictures of them on the plane?"

"It would probably cause an unholy commotion. But," he said, shrugging, "you're the expert."

Kate made a dismissing sound and stared out the window. Max had taken the aisle seat presumably so he could stretch his legs out when no one was walking by.

"Kate?"

She turned back.

"Don't worry. You'll get them."

Sighing, she said, "I don't know if I even care anymore."

"I've felt that way. It'll pass."

Kate hoped so.

The serving cart arrived at their seat and Kate finally got her coffee. She waited until the cart moved on before asking Max a question. "If this feeling passes, then what are you doing here? Why aren't you out covering some war?"

"This *is* war. The Battle of the Sexes."

"Max . . ."

He squinted as he sipped the hot coffee. "How much do you know about me?"

Nothing. That's why I asked. "Sorry if your ego takes a hit, but I don't know much. I recognized your name from your Pulitzer, and vaguely remembered something about your quitting."

"I didn't quit, I retired," he corrected. Obviously, to him, it was an important distinction.

"Why?"

"Ready to move on." Max lowered the tray and set his cup on it, thus avoiding her eyes.

"Why?" she persisted.

"It's been said that I lost my nerve." He glanced toward her then away again.

As if she'd buy that. "What do *you* say?"

Max pushed his sleeve back and read his watch. "Only eight and a half more hours to avoid answering. What are my chances?"

"Slim."

He winced.

"Don't talk about it if you don't want to, but I am curious." Extremely curious, and if Max wouldn't tell her, then she'd find somebody who would.

Max stretched his legs out. "I was caught in a hotel bomb blast along with most of the other foreign journalists and photographers in Beirut. My...closest friend died. A lot of people were killed or injured. Innocent people." He fell silent.

"I'm sorry." And she was—sorry, too, that she'd pried. Anyone would quit after something like that and understandably so.

"The irony of it was that a group of us had talked a rebel gang into letting us follow them for the night. Karl wouldn't go because he thought it was too dangerous. It was, of course. My motto was, the more danger, the better the picture. For all I know, that gang set the bomb."

"Oh, no." Kate could only imagine the guilt he'd been feeling.

He dismissed her sympathy. "I don't like talking about it. Can we just say that getting out of the country was...difficult?"

"Okay." Deep behind his eyes, Kate caught a glimpse of emotion and remembered the day they sailed across the Bay of Naples and Max's comments about mined waters. She wished she and Max were close enough for him to share more of his feelings with her.

Kate craved that closeness. It was a new emotion for her and one she didn't welcome. Until she met Max, Kate had been contentedly independent.

"But I did get out," he continued. "And I got out with rolls and rolls of film. Mine, Karl's—anybody's I could find."

Something puzzled her. "But I don't remember..." She concentrated. Was this two years ago? Three? Why didn't she remember the story? About to ask more, she stopped when she saw the bitterness on Max's face.

"You don't remember because there isn't anything *to* remember." His fist clenched around the foam coffee cup. Kate expected to see it crack. "After all I went through to get the film out, after Karl *died* covering this story, my editor wouldn't publish the pictures because they were too 'inflammatory'."

"Didn't you take them to another newspaper?"

"Remember, I worked for the wire service. They wouldn't release the pictures to the newspapers because the government asked them not to. Apparently there was a tenuous cease-fire they felt would be threatened by my pictures."

"That's censorship!" Kate was outraged on his behalf.

"Yes." Max was silent a moment. "Karl died, and I risked my life, and they wouldn't release the damn pictures. I walked."

"With the negatives?"

Max shot her a look. "What do you think?"

"I think you've got pictures nobody's seen."

"Smart girl."

At his approving look, a warmth spread through her. "Was that the first time you'd been censored?"

"Oh—" Max idly etched designs on his empty cup "—I'd been edited. I always pushed the limit with my pictures."

Everything began to fall into place. "You quit because you didn't want to be censored, is that right?"

For a moment, Kate thought he wouldn't answer, but at last, he nodded slightly.

"Does it bother you that some people think you lost your nerve, as you put it?" she asked.

"Anybody who counts knows the score." Max reclined his seat and closed his eyes, obviously weary of the discussion.

Kate sipped her lukewarm coffee and left him to his thoughts. She could just imagine his fury and frustration. She also understood the appeal of photographing for the tabloids. No holds barred. Anything goes. *No censorship*.

It was good that Max was working *with* her instead of against her on this trip.

He would be a formidable competitor.

Max returned to his charming self as the meal was served. He and Kate traded stories of their greatest triumphs, each trying to outdo the other until Max declared a tie.

Though pleased, Kate knew her shots of movie stars could in no way compare to Max's pictures and what he'd been through to get them out. Being chased by dogs was one thing, being chased by angry people with loaded guns was something else.

The plane cabin was darkened and the movie started. Soft rustlings indicated that the other passengers were settling down to sleep or putting on headphones.

"I gotta do it." Max slapped his knees.

"What?"

"Break the tie." He winked at her, then stood and rummaged in the overhead compartment, withdrawing his camera bag.

"Max?"

With a wicked look, he started for the first-class compartment. "I'm going to get them."

"Max, no! They'll hear your camera!"

"Not if they're wearing headphones."

The only reason Kate didn't stop him was because if *he* were caught, she'd still be able to follow Damian and Fiona off the plane while Max dealt with the authorities.

He had nothing to lose. Kate, however, still had hopes of surprising a jet-lagged Fiona and Damian. Also, she thought, *nobody* looked good after a transcontinental flight. She'd love to add some pictures of Fiona looking haggard to her portfolio. Later, Glen could dress them up with headlines like Fiona Ferguson, Showing The Strain Of Her Illicit Affair With Damian Carney, or Star's Looks Ruined By Lust.

The flight attendants were busy in the rear of the plane. A shadowy Max pretended to search for a magazine from the rack just to the side of the dividing curtains. Using the corner of a magazine, he parted the material. Quickly, he dropped the magazine, shoved his camera lens into the first-class compartment and pressed the shutter.

From several rows back, Kate heard the telltale click and whir of the motor, but she wasn't wearing headphones. She held her breath and looked at their fellow passengers. No one appeared to be paying any attention to Max.

Within moments, he was back and sliding into the seat. A flight attendant from first class stepped through the curtains. Max shielded his camera with his magazine. Kate pretended to watch the movie. The attendant passed by them, sweeping her gaze from side to side, her hand touching the seat backs as she walked.

"Did you get a good picture?" Kate breathed.

"Well, they weren't naked." Max winked.

He was impossible.

How would she ever live without seeing him again?

Kate asked herself that question more and more often as they approached New York. What would happen after they landed? Would Max stay with her? She wanted to ask, but couldn't find a casual way to do so.

As the plane taxied on the runway, Kate gathered her camera bag. "I'm going to pretend to be sick," she whispered to Max. "I'll run off the plane and try to ambush Fiona."

Max looked skeptical, but moved his legs out of the way.

The plane reached the gate, and Kate, hand covering her mouth, climbed over Max, pushed past the flight attendants and raced up the jetway. Once there, she waited. Sure enough, the first-class passengers debarked prior to the regular passengers.

And there was Fiona, her red hair subdued in a braid.

"Fiona!" Kate shouted and caught the actress's startled expression.

With Kate shooting rapidly, Fiona and Damian ducked and ran. When Kate saw two men in Fiona's entourage break away from the group and start for her, she ran to the nearest customs inspector, half-expecting the men to come after her. Apparently deciding she wasn't worth the trouble, they glared at her a few moments, allowing Fiona and Damian to disappear into the VIP area, then turned away.

At least she'd caught Fiona and Damian together, Kate thought, relishing the memory of Fiona's face. Fiona had probably thought Kate was still stuck in the villa gardens on Capri.

Kate didn't see Max until she finished passing through customs. When she exited, she spotted him leaning against the end of the hallway, his battered satchel at his feet.

"Did they give you a hard time about going to Italy and not shopping?" he asked.

Kate laughed. "I can't believe I was in Italy for almost two weeks and didn't buy anything other than food."

"Did you catch Fiona?"

She nodded happily. "She looked frazzled and guilty. It was great."

"She looked guilty?"

"Okay, not really, but she will when Glen finishes with the picture."

"Is that where you're going now—back to Los Angeles?"

"Yes," Kate said and risked asking, "how about you?"

"Eventually, I guess." He swung his satchel over his shoulder and fell into step beside her. "As long as I find myself in New York, I'm going to look up some friends."

Feeling disappointed, Kate nodded again. It was what she'd expected, and of course, it was for the best.

Max had already lost what brief interest he'd felt for her. For a while, on the plane, she'd hoped . . . But now they'd landed. It was time to go their separate ways.

She imagined Max making and abandoning a series of friendships and alliances fueled by the intense circumstances in which they were formed. Without the outer pressure to sustain them, such associations crumbled.

Besides, she and Max were the two least likely people to build any kind of sustained intimate relationship—

assuming Max wanted to. It would be hard enough with one of them traveling all the time, but both of them?

Knowing Max, he'd probably try hunting celebrities for a few months, especially if she left *World Eye*. Then some magazine would lure him out of his self-imposed retirement. He'd long for the prestige and the important challenges and, one day, he'd pack his bag and take off.

While waiting for her, he must have realized all this. Not flying to Los Angeles with her was his way of gently breaking off, not that there was really anything to break off.

Only in Kate's mind. Only in her heart.

"Kate?"

Kate smiled up at him, hoping she was keeping her feelings hidden.

"Will you tail Fiona to Texas?"

She shrugged. "Depends on what Glen wants."

"Make him pay for it." Max walked with her to the trains that would take them from the international terminal to the main terminal.

"Do you want me to wait with you until you catch a flight out?" he offered.

Looking at the long lines filled with summer travelers, Kate sighed. "Who knows when that'll be?" Determined to send him off with a smile no matter how much it hurt, she forced down the lump in her throat and held out her hand for him to shake.

"What's this?" he asked, taking her in his arms.

During his kiss, Kate felt her eyes burn with tears. If he didn't leave soon, she'd humiliate herself by crying.

"I *will* call you," he vowed.

Yeah, sure.

He walked backward for a few steps, then turned abruptly and strode toward the terminal exit. Kate smiled as wide as she could and waved long after her tears had blurred his figure.

Kate waited at JFK airport for hours and hours. She'd booked one flight, only to have it canceled. By the time she dragged herself into the *World Eye* offices, it was the next day. She'd slept in fits and spurts and had only stopped by her apartment long enough to drop off her bag, bathe and check the refrigerator for sour milk. Why did she buy milk anyway? she asked herself as she flushed it down the sink. She was rarely around long enough to drink it while it was fresh.

Digging her film out of her equipment bag, she decided against developing it at her apartment and headed for *World Eye.*

"Where have you been?" demanded Glen as soon as he saw her.

"Italy."

Glen was usually in a temper. Today was no exception. "Italy," he repeated in a whiny voice. "I know you've been in Italy! I want to know where you've been since yesterday."

"At JFK trying to get a flight back." Drat. The red light over the darkroom was on, indicating that someone was using the room. Now she'd have to listen to Glen's ranting and raving. It didn't bode well for the rest of the day, especially when she had some ranting of her own to do.

"Come on! Planes fly from New York to Los Angeles all the time!" Glen's pasty white skin had taken on a ruddy hue, which actually improved his appearance.

"So do people." Over Glen's shoulder, Kate watched as Angie, his underappreciated secretarial slave made a face and slipped on headphones plugged into her tape player.

"You know what I think?" Glen took three steps toward her, invading her personal space. "I think you were trying to peddle your pictures to somebody else."

Accusations like this one always kept Kate on the defensive. It was Glen's standard maneuver, she'd come to realize. And it was effective. By the time she and Glen agreed to terms, she felt grateful for the sale.

But that was before she'd met Max.

"It would serve you right if I did."

Glen's eyes narrowed. "What's that supposed to mean?"

He was close enough for her to smell the coffee on his breath. Kate consciously stopped herself from stepping backward. "Maxwell Hunter."

"What about him?"

"You sent him after me."

"I sent him after Fiona Ferguson."

"You sent *me* after Fiona Ferguson!" *Stop whining, Kate.*

"I can send anybody I want after Fiona Ferguson!"

Kate picked up her bag. "And I'm free to sell my pictures to *Global Celebrity*." It was pure bluff. Glen loathed *Global Celebrity*. His greatest nightmare was that they would scoop him. He'd let it be known that anyone who sold to the rival tabloid would never sell to him. Frankly, Kate didn't want to continue selling to second-rate tabloids. Besides, *Global Celebrity* might insist that she sign an exclusive contract as a condition to buying any Fiona pictures. Kate didn't want that.

Glen took another step forward, his fists planted near where his waist would be—if he had a waist. "You got pictures?"

Actually, no. Not compromising ones. But she happened to know that Max didn't, either, unless Fiona and Damian had been doing something scandalous in the first-class cabin. "I haven't developed my film yet," she answered, stalling for time. "I came here as soon as I could."

When Glen hesitated, Kate pressed her advantage. "*I* acted in good faith."

Glen must have sensed the change in her because he backed off, something he rarely did and certainly never so early in their discussions.

"While I'm waiting for the darkroom, why don't we discuss my expenses?"

At this, Glen, who had turned to pester Angie, whipped his head around. "Now wait a minute. We had a deal!"

"Yes, we did. And you broke it." Kate was amazed at herself. There was no betraying quiver in her voice. No visions of being evicted from her apartment flashing in her mind.

And, of course, no scandalous pictures. But Glen didn't seem to know that, which meant Max must not have reported in.

"I—I—I..." As his fury erupted, Glen's face turned completely red and his jowls shook. "I agreed to pay for your plane ticket!"

He ought to get his blood pressure checked, Kate thought. "Ah, but you offered Max carte blanche."

For a moment, she thought he'd literally explode, then a smile forced its way across his face. The alarming brick red faded. He even managed a laugh. "Ka-a-ate," he said, chuckling through her name. "Kate, Kate, Kate." He shook his head. "You..." He couldn't continue, taken as he was by a fit of mirth. "You think *you're* in the same class as *Maxwell Hunter*?"

As the heat fired her cheeks, Kate maintained enough presence of mind to hope that it was a becoming blush and not like the blotches that spattered Glen. She wanted this last image he had of her to be an attractive one, since she planned never to darken the doorway of *World Eye* again.

From the edge of her vision, she noted that the darkroom light winked out. Whistling heralded the occupant.

Kate slung her bag over her shoulder. "Since you're so impressed by Maxwell Hunter's credentials, you can buy *his* pictures."

The whistling stopped. "Somebody mention my name?"

CHAPTER EIGHT

"MAX!"

"I *did* hear someone mention my name." Apparently oblivious to the tension between Kate and Glen, Max stood next to Glen's desk and fanned the damp black-and-white prints he'd carried from the darkroom.

How did he get here so fast? "I thought you were visiting friends!" Kate said accusingly.

"I did." Max glanced up from the prints he studied. "Where've you been?"

Glen crossed his arms, a crafty smile replacing the one of momentary anxiety. "That's what *I* want to know."

"I've been trying to get a flight out!" Conscious she sounded a bit strident, Kate took a breath and deliberately softened her voice. "I was on standby for hours."

"I didn't have any trouble," Max commented and grabbed a magnifying glass.

"Whatcha got?" Glen tried to peer over Max's shoulder, but wasn't tall enough.

"This is the best of the lot, but I don't know...the faces..." Max shrugged.

They were ignoring her. "Hey, how did *you* get a ticket when I was told they were all sold out?"

Max surrendered the magnifying glass and prints to Glen and walked over to her.

Kate's breath caught. Darn it, look at him. Simply dressed in slacks and a shirt, with a smile just for her. That was all it took to set her heart thudding. She could feel it, pounding away in her chest, and swallowed. She was going to get hurt, she just knew it.

"On my flight, there was only one other person in first class."

"*First class*?" She looked from him to Glen. Glen was squinting at the pictures. "You flew first class?" She enunciated carefully, in case Glen was eavesdropping.

Max regarded her, a half smile tilting his mouth. "Frequent flyer miles, Kate."

"Oh." But Glen probably would have paid for the ticket anyway.

Max nudged her gently on the shoulder. "Come see my plane shots of Fiona."

"Sure." Kate was still stinging from the knowledge that she'd spent a day and a half of her life stranded in an airport while Max visited with friends. And he *still* managed to beat her back to Los Angeles.

Glen's attention had been caught by one of the pictures. Tilting it so the light was better, Glen moved the magnifying glass as he studied the print.

Kate recognized that expression. There was something in the picture, not much, but an element that could be enhanced, that could be stretched. With a good computer graphics program, which *World Eye* possessed, and some creative writing, which was Glen's strength, he could make something scandalous out of the most innocuous photographs. He often boasted that he could make a Sunday-school picnic look like an orgy.

Well, after this, let some other photographer supply Glen with raw material. Kate had had enough.

He looked up as they approached. Smoothing his face into a reverence befitting a legend, he indicated the picture he held. "Not bad for your first time out, Max."

What? Kate stood on her toes and tried to see Max's picture. An openmouthed Fiona snoozed in her first-class seat. Funny, but not scandalous.

"Now," Glen began, "next time, it would be even better if you got Fiona and Damian side by side. Maybe she could have her head on his shoulder."

Max nodded as Kate stared aghast. *Next time*? If *she* had turned in a picture like that, Glen would have hooted her out of the office. She opened her mouth to protest, then shut it. She *was* about to turn in pictures like that.

Glen was obviously in awe of Max. Kate should use that to her advantage.

"I'm surprised Kate didn't mention that we like to catch our lovebirds together," Glen commented with deceptive mildness and a brief admonishing glance toward her.

As Max murmured a reply, Kate wanted to laugh. Glen was hurting, right in his wallet. This trip would cost him thousands and all he had were unflattering shots of a spoiled actress. On the other hand, the pictures were *extremely* unflattering.

Kate edged toward the door.

"And where do you think you're going?" Glen demanded.

"Someplace where they'll pay me."

"Glen's going to pay you," Max interceded. "Aren't you, Glen?" Max accompanied this with a jovial slap to Glen's rounded shoulders.

"Certainly—as agreed." Glen was all smiles for Max. Kate frowned.

"And what did you agree to pay for?" Max slipped in the question oh-so-casually. Kate was impressed, even though it was none of his business. She wasn't going to protest. Maybe she could learn something about negotiating.

Glen, however, did launch into an immediate, if misguided, protest. "Oh, hey, buddy, don't worry. You're covered. Kate and I have our own arrangement. She knows you're a special case. Right, Kate?"

Kate merely looked pointedly from Glen to the pictures he held.

Max spoke, "And you, naturally, pay 'special cases' more than your regular contributors?"

He was good. But she knew that already.

Glen's expression changed as he became aware that Max had set a verbal trap for him.

"Sometimes when a picture comes our way, it's a sellers' market. Kate knows that."

"A free-lancer shopping for the best price, right?"

Glen nodded, looking as though he didn't want to.

Max tapped his jaw, apparently in thought. "Now, Kate's a free-lancer. You don't have any contractual ties to *World Eye*, do you, Kate?"

Glen started to sweat, a slick sheen visible through his thinning hair. "I bought Kate's ticket up front. Sent her halfway around the world with nothing more than a verbal agreement."

"Interesting business decision, Glen."

Glen tossed the prints across Angie's desk. She still had her headphones on, but Kate would bet that the tape was turned off.

When Glen turned back to face them, it was obvious that he'd lost some of the hero worship he'd had for Max. Kate sighed faintly. After dealing with the seamier side of people, Glen had developed a seamy side himself. Max was about to discover this.

"So what is this? A shakedown?"

It was time for Kate to intercede before Max won this battle, but lost her the war. "Glen has first rights to look at the pictures, Max."

"I *own* those pictures." *And they better be good*, his expression added.

She hadn't even developed them yet. Once she did, Glen would know she and Max were bluffing.

Her eyes met Max's. *Thanks, but no thanks*, she signaled.

He got the message. "Tell you what, Glen. While Kate develops her film, we'll discuss the expenses."

Her cue. Kate walked toward the darkroom, listening as Max discussed the bills. She'd love to watch Glen's face.

She didn't dare.

"We had a fantastic piece of luck," Max was saying as she slipped into the darkroom. "Our hotel room looked directly into Fiona's..."

But we still couldn't get incriminating shots, Kate finished silently.

Turning on the amber safelight, she checked the chemical supplies. Max had left the room in pristine condition, she noted with approval. Peering into the plastic bottles, she saw that there was enough fixer, developer and stop bath to process her rolls of film.

Good. Although she'd converted the second bathroom in her apartment into a makeshift darkroom, Glen's darkroom was larger—and using his chemicals and paper saved Kate money.

She thoroughly dried the still-damp developing tanks, removed her rolls of film and selected the ones of Fiona's room at the da Vinci and the airport photos to be processed first.

Kate used high-speed film and she preferred to work in total darkness. Switching off the safelight, she opened her film and loaded the tank.

It was a procedure she'd done thousands of times before and could perform by rote. As she wound the film onto the reel, she strained to make out the conversation Max was having with Glen.

Occasionally, Glen raised his voice. Though she couldn't decipher the words, she imagined an outburst when he saw the expenses for the boat rental, the suite at the Principe and full-fare airline tickets.

The suite at the Principe would really get to him. She wished she could see his face. She wished she could *hear* Max's explanation.

Kate closed the cover of the developing tank and switched on the safelight.

Checking to see that the developer was at the correct temperature, she poured it into the tank. Occasionally shaking it to assure that her film developed properly, Kate wandered over to the negative strips hanging from a line stretched across the room.

Max had been here awhile. He'd had enough time to print contact sheets, and select and enlarge the best pictures.

He hadn't exposed many rolls of film, Kate noted.

She carefully studied the automatic exposures his camera had taken of Fiona's suite.

Incredibly, there was only one picture with Fiona and Damian in the same frame. This was obviously just after Damian had arrived and Fiona had let him into the room. In it, Fiona was walking away from the door, Damian following her. They weren't even touching.

Kate checked the second hand on her watch and sighed. During the time Max's camera had made that shot, Max himself was with her at the car, trying to convince her to come up to the room. Maybe if she hadn't been so hardheaded and had *listened* to him, she could have taken a picture of Damian and Fiona kissing each other in greeting.

No, she knew better than to dwell on what might have been. Fiona had been angry about being sent to Texas. She hadn't been in a loving mood.

Kate poured the developer back into the bottle and added stop bath to the tank. After a minute, she poured the stop bath down the drain and replaced it with fixer.

She had a few more minutes before she had to rinse everything off. Periodically agitating the tank, Kate pressed her ear to the darkroom door.

Max and Glen were still talking. There was an occasional burst of laughter, which meant that they'd finished the touchy money talks.

She couldn't stand it. Pouring out the fixer, she added neutralizer, waited impatiently, then poured it back into the jar and set the tank in the sink. Turning on the tap and leaving the tank in running water, Kate practically burst through the darkroom door.

Max and Glen looked at her in surprise.

"Did you get something?" Glen asked too eagerly.

Kate hooked a thumb over her shoulder. "Still washing off." She glanced at Max and tried to read his expression.

His expression was smug. "Before things get crazy around here, Glen, why don't you have Angie cut Kate her expense check? I took the liberty of discussing the figures with Glen while you were in the darkroom," he explained to Kate as though she'd had absolutely no idea what he'd been up to.

Angie whipped out the checkbook before Glen could say anything. Not that he would. Max was clearly the one in charge here and they all knew it.

With mixed emotions, Kate watched Angie type the check for Glen's signature. On one hand, she hated talking money with Glen. On the other, she hated having Max do the dirty work for her. It made her appear weak. And Kate didn't want to appear weak, not in front of Glen and not in front of Max.

With little grace, Glen scrawled his signature on the check. Just before she accepted it, Kate remembered

Max's words: *I promise you won't take a financial hit because of me.*

She glanced at the amount. He was a man of his word.

She couldn't look at him, even though she knew he expected some sort of grateful reaction from her. "Thanks, Glen. I'll go sponge off the film."

He and Max followed her into the darkroom, barely allowing her to hang the damp strips before pouncing on them.

Glen immediately found the frames of Fiona and Damian on the couch. "Ah, Kate!" He swallowed whatever stronger expletive he'd been going to say, probably in deference to Max's presence. "We can't break the story without their faces showing!"

She'd realized that. "But we do know that they're having an affair. Before this, we only suspected. *And*, Max and I were the only photographers around. No one else has a clue."

"How long is *that* going to last?" Glen glared at both of them and turned back to the negatives.

"Sooner or later, she'll get careless," Kate said and pointed to the photos of Fiona on the telephone. "*Roman Vengeance* is shooting interiors in Texas, just north of Houston. Fiona is furious. Look at her."

"Hmm."

Kate knew Glen was thinking of possibilities. Glen always thought of possibilities.

Max spoke. "How about sending Kate to Texas?"

She had been about to suggest that very thing. She'd *wanted* to suggest that very thing, but Max had beaten her to it. She shot him an angry look, which he returned with a puzzled frown. Her frustration grew. Max must think she was a complete incompetent.

Glen dropped the negatives and shook his head. "I'll *have* to send Kate to Texas. I've got too much invested in this Fiona story to quit now."

"I'll get right on it," Kate said, relieved she'd get another chance.

"I don't need to tell you what I'm looking for," Glen said, then proceeded to do just that. "I need a *defining* photo. I need Fiona and Damian playing kissy face. Then I can run this other stuff."

Kate hoped the amber light in the darkroom hid the blush she felt. A lecture in front of Max. Now her humiliation was complete.

But it wasn't, she discovered. Max defended her. "Glen, Fiona is being very cagey. She knows her career is at stake with this movie."

Max sounded like *he* was the Fiona expert. Kate's anger turned to resentment. There was Glen, nodding and agreeing with everything Max said. Max could do no wrong. Max was worth first-class treatment and don't spare the expense.

Max was turning her life upside down.

"Damian has taught her a few tricks..."

That did it. As she heard her own words coming from Max, Kate stormed out of the darkroom.

Max defending her. How lowering. And Glen looking serious and nodding his agreement, when Kate knew if *she'd* said the exact same words, he wouldn't have paid the slightest attention. But because it was *Max*...

As soon as she could, Kate retrieved the rest of her undeveloped rolls of film and left the *World Eye* office for her apartment, fuming all the way. It wouldn't surprise her to find a message from Glen on her answering machine telling her he'd given *Max* the Fiona-in-Texas assignment.

Kate stopped off at the bank to cash Glen's check on her way home. She'd have a roof over her head for another month, so she supposed she should be grateful to Max.

But she wasn't.

In the next hour, Kate paid her landlady, gathered her dirty laundry and dragged it down to the apartment complex's laundry room.

Climbing the stairs on the way back to her second-story apartment, she wasn't really surprised to find Max lounging against the railing of her tiny balcony.

"Glen told you where I lived, right?" she said by way of greeting.

He straightened. "No, I memorized your address from your passport."

Good grief. Kate unlocked the door, wishing she could avoid letting Max inside.

"Kate?" Max touched her arm. "You're angry. I'd like to know why. Could we..." He gestured to her apartment.

Kate met his eyes, gray eyes with tiny lines at the corners, and was lost. If he'd assumed he could come in or if he'd been accusatory, she would have snapped at him.

But no. He was reasonable and mature.

As she opened her door, she wasn't quite so angry and found herself resenting him for it. Did he have to be perfect?

She watched him glance around her small apartment, striding at once to the wall where she'd framed and hung some of her favorite photographs. They were just pictures of people she'd encountered, usually taken when they weren't aware of Kate and her camera.

She held her breath and watched for Max's reaction. It was the first time she'd ever had anyone who knew photography in her living room.

In fact, she rarely entertained anyone at all.

Conscious of her duties as hostess, Kate broke the silence. "Would you like something to drink?" Then she panicked, wondering if she *had* anything to drink.

Obviously concentrating on her photos, Max murmured something unintelligible, which Kate took as an assent.

She opened the refrigerator. Milk was out. Likewise orange juice. Not even a can of soda. Opening the freezer, she saw that the ice-cube trays were wearing white beards.

Perhaps something hot.

The best she could manage was an ancient jar of instant coffee and she had to struggle to twist off the lid.

She hoped Max took his coffee black.

He was still studying her pictures. A nervous Kate managed to spoon coffee into mugs, added tap water and shoved them into the microwave.

Why didn't he say something? Did he think her people pictures were goofy? Did he wonder why she'd framed them? Did he find them amateurish? Unworthy?

Max's opinion suddenly took on an immense importance.

The microwave dinged and Kate removed the mugs, gave the coffee a final stir and walked into her living room.

"Here's your coffee."

"Thanks." He took it without looking at her.

Kate's hands shook and she sipped at her coffee to keep it from sloshing over the rim of the mug.

It was lukewarm and tasted horrible, especially after the wonderfully full-bodied cappuccinos of Italy.

Max took a sip before she could warn him. "You're good," he said. "The coffee isn't."

He waved off Kate's apology and headed for the kitchen. "Somehow, I thought all you did was chase celebrities." Setting his mug in the microwave, he heated the coffee for a few seconds. "But the expressions and emotions you captured in the faces of those people... You could be a portrait artist, you know?"

Kate exhaled in a whoosh. "Really?"

Nodding, Max removed his cup from the microwave. "I feel as if I know those people. As if I know their stories."

"So do I," Kate admitted shyly.

But she didn't admit that she sometimes talked to her pictures, that after she'd enlarged and framed the prints of people, her apartment never seemed empty.

Max sat on her small, two-cushion sofa, completely dwarfing the piece. "You work primarily in black and white, don't you?"

"Yes." Kate sat in the only other chair—a stark, black-metal framed "designer" piece that she thought added class to her apartment.

Class was the only thing it added, as she immediately discovered that it was horribly uncomfortable. Had she ever sat in it before? Had anyone?

Max's eyes lit with amusement, which flustered her. Obviously, there wasn't much he missed. "Have you thought of going into portraiture full-time?"

Yes, she had, but she felt shy telling him. "I'd have to establish a studio and there would be a start-up period when I wouldn't have any income."

Wrapping both hands around the mug, Max leaned forward. "Couldn't you continue free-lancing while you set up your business?"

"Yes, but as a very erratic supplement. I wouldn't have the time to maintain my contacts, so it's important that I have a financial cushion." Kate gulped the nasty-tasting coffee and confessed, "I'm hoping that Fiona's picture will give me that cushion."

Mentioning Fiona reminded Kate that she was angry with Max. "Speaking of Fiona—"

"What's bothering you?"

Kate gritted her teeth in annoyance. There he was taking the lead again. "While I appreciate your efforts in getting Glen to reimburse me—"

"I got you a per diem, too." He grinned.

"I noticed. I've already spent it." After hesitating, she added a gruff "Thanks."

"You're welcome."

"It's just that I would have preferred to negotiate with him myself. What am I going to do when I've finally got the picture and you aren't around?"

"What makes you think I'm not going to be around?"

Kate's breath caught. "Because...are you going to Texas?"

"Yes."

Kate's heart picked up speed. Was she glad or not? Glad in the short run, but wouldn't it hurt more when they did part for good? "To stalk Fiona?"

"After she proved so elusive in Italy, I'd like to see you get your picture." He drained his mug and set it on the coffee table. "So how about it? Want a temporary partner?"

Kate heard "temporary". Struggling to sort her feelings into a response, she set her mug next to his. "I...it's important to me—very important—that *I* be the one to photograph Fiona."

"I remember," he reassured her. "Will you let me help you?"

Kate spread her hands. "If you want to."

"I want to." Max regarded her for a moment, then stood. "How fast can you pack?"

"Fast, but I've got wet laundry."

"Take care of your laundry. I'll make plane reservations."

There he was, taking charge again. Kate made her token protest. "You don't have to come to Texas with me."

"I don't see why not." Max reached for the telephone. "I live in Texas."

CHAPTER NINE

IN JULY, Houston was an inferno.

Kate immediately realized her all-black wardrobe was a mistake. Pants were a mistake. *Clothes* were a mistake.

And it appeared that Houston in July was a monumental mistake. No wonder Fiona was angry.

The soundstages at The Woodlands, a tiny community north of the actual city, were shaded by tall pines, but shade provided only marginal relief in the sticky heat.

Kate had followed her usual procedure—find where Fiona spent her off-hours and camp nearby. But the ground was squishy and the mosquitoes were delighted to make her acquaintance. She'd spent the entire morning suffering and was about to abandon her stakeout. She, who had successfully battled cold, wet, hunger and boredom, was surrendering to the Houston heat.

To top it off, she was hallucinating. From her spot on the edge of an asphalt parking lot, she watched cars come and go. Moments earlier, a Range Rover had pulled into a parking place and its driver emerged. To Kate's heat-addled brain, the man, wreathed in shimmering heat waves, was Max. Or a vision she imagined was Max. She hadn't seen or heard from Max since they'd parted at the airport.

He said he'd call and he knew her hotel, but after three days, she'd quit pestering the front desk for messages.

He haunted her thoughts, her dreams.

She missed him.

The vision scanned the area and she saw its lips move. "Kate?"

Wonderful. Auditory hallucinations, too. Was that a symptom of heatstroke?

"I know you're out here, Kate. And if you don't tell me where, I'm going to make a lot of noise and attract attention to myself."

That sounded *a lot* like Max. She groaned.

He must have heard the small sound, because he turned at once in her direction. Quickly spotting her, he strode toward her carefully concealed spot.

"Hi." Without ceremony, he plopped an insulated cooler in front of her and sat on it.

"You're blocking my view," Kate grumbled.

"That's because I want you to look at me."

"Okay, so I'm looking." She looked. He looked good. And with his loose-fitting khaki slacks and white cotton shirt, he looked cool, as well.

"Aren't you glad to see me, Kate?" he prompted.

"I don't know. Where's your camera?"

"I left it with the concierge at your hotel. Nice to see Glen is putting you up at some better places."

A reluctant grin crossed her face. "Fiona is staying there."

"I know."

Honestly, Max knew everything.

"Are you wondering why I haven't called you?"

"Max!" She fiddled with her camera strap. It was hard to avoid his gaze since he was sitting right in front of her.

He nudged her leg with his toe. "You were supposed to wonder. That was the plan."

She glared at him. "I don't like playing games."

"I remember. You take everything very seriously." His smile faded. "So did I, once."

As Kate started to ask him what he meant, Max interrupted her. "The reason I didn't call—"

"You don't have to explain," she hurriedly interrupted *him*. She wanted to pretend she'd been so busy she'd lost track of the time. He wouldn't be fooled, though.

"But I told you I'd call. And I'd intended to."

He sounded irritated, so Kate let him speak.

"I live way out in the country and my power cable broke while I was gone. I lost everything in the refrigerator."

"Ugh." Kate made a face as she imagined smells a hundred times worse than her sour milk.

"Also, my only telephone is a cordless one—big mistake. It needs electricity. So no phone. No power. That's what I've been up to."

Kate slapped another mosquito. "Sounds like you've had just as much fun as I've had."

"That's about to change." Abruptly, Max stood and pried the lid off the cooler. "I brought you a present."

Whatever it was, it was cold. Max waved aside the fog that billowed out of the container.

Kate saw an assortment of small frosted cartons. "Ice cream!" Nothing, except snow, could be more welcome.

"You'll now reveal the secrets of your personality by the flavor you choose." Max sat on the ground. "So, will it be plain vanilla? Chocolate? Strawberry cheesecake?"

Kate bit her lip and blinked up at him. "All three?"

"I see you have a many-faceted personality." Max laughed and handed her a spoon. "Go for it."

Kate would have responded, but her mouth was full of ice cream.

Max selected a carton—chocolate, Kate noticed—and pulled off the cardboard top.

She'd wolfed down half of hers before he'd taken a bite. "Thanks. I didn't know how I was going to last through the afternoon. In fact," she admitted, "I was about to call it quits."

"Good, because I've come to drag you off to my lair."

"What?"

"My home," he clarified. "I'm inviting you to see my house."

"I'd like that." Kate was touched. She'd caught a note in his voice that told her it wasn't a casual invitation.

"Great." He gestured to her spoon. "We'll leave as soon as you're finished."

Lost in the sensation of cold sliding down her throat, Kate's heat-soaked mind didn't immediately sift through Max's words.

His intention finally registered when he fitted the lid back on the cooler instead of offering her more ice cream.

"Right now?" she asked.

His mouth tilted with amusement. "Aren't you miserable in this heat?"

"*Yes*." She lifted her ponytail and fanned her neck.

"You know Fiona better than I do, but do you honestly think she's going to set foot outside the air-conditioning with or without Damian?"

Max was right. Kate knew he was right. He was always right, darn it.

"She may not," Kate answered coolly, no mean accomplishment in this heat, "but I *know* she won't be at your house."

Max opened her bag and started packing. Kate hated it when someone else touched her camera equipment and tugged it out of his reach.

He didn't seem bothered at all. "No, because she's attending a local fund-raiser this evening."

"Where?"

"Hawthorne Gallery."

"How'd you find out?"

"Since Fiona wants to be noticed, I figured she'd try to keep a high profile while she's here. So I dropped by the *Post*," he said, referring to Houston's morning newspaper, "and chatted with the society columnists."

Kate wished she'd thought of that. She *should* have thought of that. "And?"

He shrugged modestly. "I've got copies of the press releases her people have sent out."

"She posted a public appearance schedule?"

"For, ah, photo opportunities. Approved ones, naturally, but I thought we'd at least know where she was."

Kate closed her eyes. Tightly. She'd lost her touch. After this assignment, she might as well retire to become a clerk in a one-hour photo developing booth.

"Kate?"

She opened her eyes, expecting to see him struggling to control his mirth.

But Max wasn't laughing. "If you'd prefer, I can drive you out some other time." There was a stiffness, a hint of something behind his words. If Kate didn't know better, she'd think it was uncertainty.

It reminded her of how she'd felt when he'd entered her apartment; how she'd wondered what his reaction would be to her photographs. How much his opinion mattered to her.

Now she realized that *her* opinion of his home mattered to him. "I'd love to see your home," she said with extra enthusiasm.

She was rewarded with a blinding smile.

"Good," he said, and extended a hand. "It's a two-hour drive each way, but I'll have you back in time to catch Fiona at the gallery."

Kate grasped Max's hand and stood, swiping pine needles from her pants. "If we make it back in time, fine, and if we don't, then Fiona will just have to get along without me."

"Do you mean that?" Max asked, gazing at her intently.

And with a sense of wonder, Kate realized she truly did.

Max's home was in the fertile central Texas area near Brenham. Kate's impression was of a lush green country with homes on generous acreage. It was popular with older couples who'd retired, Max informed her, being out in the country but close enough to Houston to offer the excitement of a large metropolitan area.

What was Max doing living all the way out here?

They turned off the main highway, passed through a spare iron arch and rumbled over a well-worn dirt road.

He pulled the Range Rover into the circle drive and parked in front of a native-stone house shaded by a live oak tree. Max's home was modest by comparison with some of the stately houses she'd seen, and fitted in more with the rolling landscape than the others.

Hauling out the cooler and slamming the door shut, he brought his finger to his lips. "Listen."

Kate didn't hear anything and said so.

"That's right." Max beamed. "Silence." He scanned the area, a contented smile on his face. "That's what attracted me to this property. It's peaceful and quiet. And green."

And lonely, Kate thought, absently pulling at a young, denuded bush.

"Deer," Max said with a frown. "They've been treating my landscaping attempts like an all-you-can-eat buffet."

Deer in his front yard. What a difference from New York or Los Angeles. "What do you do out here all day long?" Kate asked as he fitted a key into the front door. "Other than feed the deer?"

He smiled, shaking his head. "When I bought this place a year ago, it was in bad shape. I've done most of the renovations myself."

Kate heard the pride in his voice, along with something else. "You sound surprised." She stepped across the threshold, mentally composing something complimentary in case he wasn't as accomplished a renovator as he was a photographer.

"I am. I had no idea what I was getting into—and would probably never do it again," he added with a rueful laugh.

Kate didn't need her prepared speech. "It's gorgeous!" she blurted out when she saw the soaring ceiling and the two-story stone fireplace. "You did this *yourself*?"

"Yes." Pointing, he said, "I raised the ceiling into the attic and extended the fireplace using stone from an outside wall I knocked out. The stone had weathered and didn't match, so I had to clean it. Then it was *too* clean and I had to scrub the fireplace . . ." He shoved his hands into his back pockets, his gaze following the line of the fireplace. "It's not perfect, but it's pretty good."

"Perfect is boring," Kate said promptly, running her hands over the glossy wooden guardrail surrounding the sunken living room. She could almost feel the heat left by his hands polishing the wood with endless strokes.

"I worked with an architect to add on the studio. When I ran into rough spots, I'd hire some craftsmen for a few days, but . . ." He lifted a shoulder. "It kept me busy for the past year."

"Did you need to be kept busy?" Kate asked carefully.

His hand had followed hers across the railing, pausing to rub at a tiny bubble in the varnish. Sighing, he answered her. "I was thrown by the reaction of my publisher to the hotel bombing. I couldn't... accept the censorship, or the cover-up. Or the fact that it might be years before the truth comes out." He turned to her. "And it might never." Looking off into the distance, out the windows lining the living area, he drew a long breath. "I couldn't handle it." His voice had dropped to a broken whisper.

Feeling helplessly inadequate, Kate covered the hand that still gripped the railing with her own. They stood there for some moments, Max still staring outside, seeing unknown sights, reliving unknown fears.

"Show me the rest of the house?" she asked when the silence stretched too long.

"Sure." Max visibly pulled himself back to the present with a strained smile. "There're two bedrooms, this living area and through here is the studio." He pointed, then gestured for her to walk ahead of him.

The studio was as big as the main living area.

"The darkroom is over there," he said, hands back in his pockets, as if for some reason he had to restrain himself.

Kate pushed open the door. A stainless-steel sink gleamed and pristine developing paraphernalia sat on the counters. Plastic bottles of unmixed chemicals lined the shelves. There were no rings on the shelves, no old drips down the sides of the bottles. No stains on the white vinyl floor.

She inhaled. Sheetrock. Sawdust. Paint.

The room had never been used.

"It's state of the art." Max's voice sounded hollow.

Kate shot him a look. "And you have nothing to develop."

"That'll change," he said after a beat.

She studied Max's face, but his expression was as closed as a shutter.

The studio was a photographer's dream. Lots and lots of natural light—north light, Kate surmised. Platforms, light tables, umbrellas and blackout curtains. Everything was there. Everything except photographs.

The walls were bare, both in the studio and in the rest of his home. To Kate, that was an ominous sign.

"I need to put the ice cream into the freezer," Max said before leaving her alone.

Couldn't he stand to stay in the studio? Were the memories it evoked too painful? After a moment, Kate followed him into a smallish kitchen.

He barely glanced at her. "Soft drink?" he offered after emptying the cooler.

"Anything cold and wet." She wouldn't even specify a diet cola.

Kate was aware of an awkwardness between them. Guessing it had to do with his pictures, or the lack of them, she broached the issue. "I'd like to see some of your work."

His back was toward her as he poured her drink, but Kate saw him flinch. Surely he expected to show her his work. Why else would he bring her all the way out here?

"There's an album in the bookcase. I was the official photographer for my parent's fortieth wedding anniversary," he said, and handed her the glass.

Family photos. That was a good start, Kate thought, but they both knew what work she really wanted to see.

He obviously wasn't ready. In the meantime, she'd enjoy seeing Max's family.

"Where is this?" she asked, noticing that several men wore cowboy boots with their suits.

"Austin. That's my brother Matt and my niece and nephew." Max continued pointing out various relatives and friends, each person prompting a story, which he shared with her.

For Kate, time stopped. Sitting next to him on the overstuffed sofa, she eagerly soaked in Max's past, mentally comparing it with her own. Like Max, she resembled her mother more than her father. In Max's case, it was the eyes, an arresting gray that his brother didn't have. In Kate's case, it was her build. She was petite, but stronger than she appeared. The runt, as her brothers and sisters were fond of saying.

Kate came from a farm family. Max's family had worked in oil and had traveled and lived all over the world.

Kate envied Max's eclectic childhood; he envied her lifelong childhood friends.

"So now you know all there is to know about me," Max said, closing the album.

"I doubt it." She knew Max's childhood past. She knew his present, but she didn't know all that went into molding Max into the man he was.

His photojournalistic work might hold the answers and Kate intended to find out.

"You've seen my work. May I see yours?"

She could tell he'd been prepared for her request.

A jaw muscle tensed, but his voice was even. "If you're ready."

He was the one who needed to be ready, Kate thought. "Are your pictures that awful?"

He gestured around them. "I don't take the sort of photographs one displays on walls."

Like she did. Embarrassment fired her face.

"Kate." Max slid an arm around her shoulders and gave her a gentle shake. "I didn't mean anything against your work. I just..." He swallowed. "Come with me."

Max led the way back into the studio and straight to the cabinets lining the end of the oblong room. He hesitated, then jerked open a double door.

Jumbled inside, at odds with the immaculate room, were boxes, albums, file folders and proof sheets. Max, seemingly at random, began emptying the shelves.

Kate knew there were hundreds—thousands—of photographs.

Max moved like a man possessed.

She said nothing as he continued from one cabinet to the next, dumping boxes on the floor so hard they tilted over, spilling their contents.

Max reached the last cabinet and froze, then slowly shut the door on a single carton, leaving it inside.

And that was the carton Kate knew she most wanted to see.

Chest heaving, Max turned his back and leaned against the door, head bowed, hands drawn to his waist.

Say something. Kate stood next to the worktable and prayed for the right words, but her mind was blank.

Max pierced her with a look, then silently and inexplicably strode from the studio.

After remaining motionless for countless seconds, Kate knelt by one of the spilled boxes and fanned out the black-and-white prints. Some curled at the edges, as though their developing had been hastened.

Kate had no idea how long she spent in Maxwell Hunter's brand-new studio becoming shocked, horrified, saddened and angry by his pictures of human beings in conflict.

Straightening the mess as she went along, Kate worked her way to the closed cabinet at the end. Whether he returned or not, she knew she'd eventually look in that box, but after what she'd just seen, Kate didn't think she could be any more shocked or repulsed.

Max's pictures held a raw power that said much about the man who had exposed himself to danger to take them. He was talented and fearless, a formidable combination.

And he couldn't be allowed to quit now.

The light outside the windows changed. Shadows lengthened and Kate was aware of her empty stomach.

She wasn't hungry.

She'd reached the closed cabinet.

Kate tugged open the door and stared at the un-marked box. Before she could change her mind, she dragged it off the shelf, dropped it onto the floor and pried off the top.

In contrast to the other photographs, these prints were all the same size and filed neatly. No curling edges. Kate pulled at a section near the middle.

"No!" The harsh command echoed like a shot in the empty room.

Kate started, dropping the pictures.

Max, radiating anger, hurried toward her.

Jumping to her feet, she faced him. "Didn't you expect me to look at those? *Didn't you*?" she accused him in a voice as sharp as his.

"I—" With both hands, he covered his eyes as if to block out memories, then raked his fingers through his hair and groaned. "I changed my mind."

"Why?"

"Some of those photographs aren't meant to be seen." He stooped and replaced the pictures she'd dropped.

"Because they're of your last assignment? The bombing? The trip through mined waters?"

Max didn't answer. He fitted the lid back on the box as if he were boxing off the memories, as well.

Kate knelt. "Max."

His movements stilled and he faced her, his eyes dull. Was he protecting her? Or himself?

"Tell me," she said simply.

Looking infinitely older, he shifted until he sat on the floor, linking his arms around his knees, facing the purpling dusk.

Kate sat, too, registering the coolness of the tiled floor. Max didn't speak at once and Kate was prepared to wait as long as necessary. She felt he was ready to share his experiences with someone and that he knew it was time he did so, but the realization didn't make the telling any easier.

"*International Journal* invited me to submit works for a photojournalists' retrospective," he began on a sigh. "Invitations like that aren't unusual, but this one was going to be a big deal and it came almost to the day I finished this place." He laughed softly. "I was going to plant vegetables next."

"I've done that," Kate said dryly.

"Right. The farm." He thought for a minute. "I just realized that there weren't any plants in your apartment."

"No animals, either."

"Don't you miss the farm?"

"No," Kate said at once. "I already told you I didn't fit in on the farm. Now tell me about the invitation," she persisted, recognizing his delaying tactics.

He drew a deep breath and thankfully abandoned farm talk. "I would have ignored the letter, but it was raining that day and..."

"So you started going through your pictures," she guessed.

He nodded. "I hadn't looked at any of them since I walked out of the syndicate offices." His voice lost the contemplative tone and took on a harder edge. "Everything came back, including how angry I'd been. The injustice . . . the waste . . .''

Gesturing to the pictures on the floor behind him, the ones Kate had seen, he continued, ''When I looked through those, I realized that there had been several times when the most gut-wrenching photo never made it to press.''

Kate felt his pain as if it were her own. ''But think how many of them did make it into print. For the sake of argument, perhaps your editor had to pick those pictures that illustrated a broader story, rather than hardhitting, but limited.''

She could see him consider her words, rather than react defensively.

''It comes down to a matter of opinion, I know.'' He shrugged. ''I'll put my personal choices in the retrospective. But those . . .'' He tapped the closed box. ''Maybe censorship has its place. All I know is that I don't ever want to be censored again.''

''Enter celebrity photography.'' His unusual new career choice now made complete sense to Kate.

''I saw Glen's rag on the newsstand and I remember thinking, 'how can they get away with printing this stuff?' It'd been years since I worked with Glen, but I hopped a plane to L.A. Next thing I knew, I was trying to rescue one of the stubbornest women I've ever met.''

Kate grinned. ''I consider being called stubborn a compliment.''

Dusk stole the light from the studio, leaving a dimness that suited their mood. Lines of tension had relaxed around Max's mouth. Kate hoped she'd brought him some measure of peace.

Without saying anything, Max reached for her hand, lacing their fingers together.

In that moment, with the warmth of his hand entwined with hers, Kate felt closer to Max than she'd ever felt to another human being.

Her family loved her and she loved them, but they didn't understand the "differentness" they sensed in her and, except for Jonathan, never tried to.

Max understood.

And now she understood Max.

It was a heady feeling. A risky feeling. Because as close as she felt, Kate wanted to become closer.

She gazed at him in the twilight, her face unguarded.

"Kate..." It was a whisper and she knew he saw the yearning she didn't hide.

He moved closer to her, his other hand cupping the back of her head. "Kate," he whispered again before his lips met hers in a kiss, first of discovery, then growing passion.

This was a different passion from the white-hot desire that had flashed through her in the suite at the Principe. Ignited by physical attraction, it had quickly flamed and just as quickly burned out.

This passion was driven by the embers of deep emotion that Kate instinctively knew would burn within her for a long time.

She gave herself wholeheartedly, holding nothing back in her response. It was no longer a matter of choice.

Max broke the kiss to stare at her, searching her face in the growing darkness. "It took me so long to find you," he murmured, shifting closer and trailing slow kisses along the side of her neck.

And now that he'd found her, what? How long would he be content?

Shuddering, Kate sought his mouth with hers, holding him close. For now.

And it was apparent that Max needed to be held. Kate didn't know what private demons he battled, what memories he revisited, but he held her tightly, with a fierce vulnerability.

The room was completely dark by the time he released her from the circle of his arms. "Thanks." He looked down at her and Kate saw that the hard lines of his mouth had softened and the haunted look had left his eyes. "I'd like to show you the pictures now."

He meant the ones in the last box.

When Kate nodded, Max stood and turned on a small desk lamp.

She stretched her legs, stiff from the cold tile floor.

"Why don't you come over to the table," Max invited her and held out a folding chair. It didn't look much more comfortable than the floor.

"Ouch." Kate winced when she got up.

Max waited until she was seated at the table before crossing the room and returning with the closed box.

Hesitating only briefly, he removed the lid and ran his hands over the edges of the files, stopping at a fat one and removing it.

"The bombing," he said, but Kate already knew.

He let her open the folder. She was conscious that his gaze rested on her more than the pictures.

In a voice tight with suppressed emotion, he told again the story of his night with the soldiers, this time illustrated with photographs. When they reached the photos of the aftermath of the hotel explosion, his hand trembled.

"There was never anything more than a brief paragraph in the newspapers," Max said with renewed bitterness. "I still think the whole thing was a setup."

"I'm sorry," Kate said, wishing there were stronger words.

She closed the file and reached for the rest of the photographs.

Max grabbed her wrist. "Don't."

"Why not?" She'd thought they'd reached a new closeness. A trust.

"These are...civilians. Families." He cleared his throat. "Children." He swallowed. "Here, let me show you these."

He pulled out a slim folder and opened it. "This was my friend and colleague, Karl."

The first picture was of a smilingly attractive blond man. "Is he the one who was killed?"

Max nodded.

Kate saw pictures of Max and Karl together and separately, when they'd photographed each other. Glad to see lighter photos, she stopped at one of Max in front of some monument. As she looked up, intending to ask him where it was, Max blinked rapidly, his eyes glinting with extra moisture.

He answered her question, his voice steady, but in that instant, when he teared up at the memory of his lost friend, Kate fell in love with Maxwell Hunter.

She felt it, felt the exact instant her feelings of admiration, attraction and regard crystallized into a single all-encompassing love.

It was a relief to finally admit her love, but it was a short-lived relief, because at the same time, Kate realized that she could never, should never, hold on to Max.

The world needed to see his pictures. Max was a photographer of enormous talent and compassion. It was much too early for him to walk away from his photography.

He'd spent the past year healing and his restlessness now was comparable to the itch of new skin. He was ready to photograph again whether or not he admitted it. And he was ready to photograph something more substantial than a spoiled starlet and her clandestine lover.

For now though, the pursuit of Fiona and Damian would serve a dual purpose: Kate would avenge Jonathan, and Max would regain his passion for his work.

Kate vowed to help him finish healing, even though she knew that one day, Max would feel the heat of the world's hot spots and he'd return to them, leaving her behind.

CHAPTER TEN

"AT LAST, at last." Using Max's shoulder as a prop, Kate stood on tiptoe and snapped photograph after photograph of Fiona draped bonelessly across Damian's lap, her famous diamond bracelet glittering in the gallery lighting. Fiona and Damian had just posed for an authorized publicity photo, and Fiona had decided to stay on his lap.

For ten days, Kate and Max had followed Fiona from one Houston night spot to another. There were plays, symphony performances, late-night dinners and a charity tennis tournament—all dutifully recorded by Kate, though for the first time, she felt a part of the events instead of merely an observer. Her change of outlook was entirely due to Max, she admitted and wondered how she could ever return to the way she used to work.

Since the time at his home, when she'd seen the pictures, Max was freer. Funny and outrageous, he dared her to take chances, urged her to participate. Instead of allowing Kate to wait on the fringes of the tennis court, Max bought tickets and two commemorative hats to shield them from the sun.

In the swarm of people around the drink stand, Max nudged Kate and she found herself standing in line behind Fiona. Fiona never turned around, to Kate's relief.

Fiona was sometimes accompanied by Damian, sometimes not, but up until tonight, Kate's photographs were innocuous.

Secretly, Kate was glad Fiona had behaved because that meant more time with Max. She mentally photographed each moment they spent together to tuck away in a scrapbook of memories. Always, she was careful to hide her feelings, keeping their time together casual and light. When Max did decide to return to his true profession, she wanted to spare him any guilt over hurting her.

She'd been back to his home several times, and together they sorted through photographs and negatives for the retrospective. After much discussion, they included several pictures of the bombing, then reprinted them, finally breaking in his darkroom. Max acted as if a tremendous weight had been removed from his conscience. The world would see his pictures at last.

Max's talent astounded her. His kisses delighted her. And each time they parted, she felt a pang she knew was a harbinger of the pain she'd feel when they parted for the final time.

Glen was beside himself at the delay, but Kate had discovered that Houston was on the travel itinerary of many notables. During the daytime, she photographed enough of them to keep Glen appeased.

Tonight all her persistence in following Fiona had paid off.

She and Max were attending a museum reception for art patrons. The stars of *Roman Vengeance* were special guests. The museum's excuse was that they were highlighting Italian artists, but Kate knew the highbrow contributors were as star struck as everyone else.

The press, while notified of the event, were not invited inside. Max, characteristically, saw that as a plus. Grumbling, Kate had prepared for a night of waiting in the oppressively muggy Houston heat—until a formally suited Max had arrived at her hotel-room door with two invitations to the reception.

"Where did you get those?" she'd demanded suspiciously, once she recovered from the impressive sight of Max in formal wear.

"Just call me a patron of the arts," he'd replied with the self-confident smile she knew so well.

"Max!" Kate stared at the cream-and-gilt invitation. "These are for the prereception!"

"Yes."

"But you have to contribute at least a thousand dollars to get invited!"

"Are you suggesting that fine art isn't worth at least that much?"

"I—" Kate broke off. There was no arguing with him when he was like this. He'd bought her this chance at Fiona, and while she appreciated it, once again she owed Max. Unless... "They're not going to let me in with my camera, are they?"

Max shrugged. "Leave your big lens here and try to look like an amateur. We'll pretend we want a souvenir picture with Fiona." His smile was back in place. "After all, it's the least they can do for someone who contributed—"

Kate covered her ears. "I don't want to know."

Laughing, Max had left her to change clothes while he waited in the lobby.

And so now, after an hour of standing around watching Fiona drink too much Asti Spumante, Kate finally had a photograph Glen could use to break the story. *Soon, Jonathan*, she vowed.

"Rats. I need to change film." She lifted her camera from Max's shoulder and he turned around to glance at the scene behind them.

"She looks like a sloshed mermaid."

"It's the green sequins." Kate moved to a shadowy corner. Max positioned himself to block as much of the light as possible while she loaded film. "Keep an eye on them for me, will you?" Kate asked.

"Gladly."

Max spoke with such enthusiasm that Kate glanced over at the scene. Fiona's wiggling had exposed even more of her bounteous cleavage than the dress intended. Innocent Italian farm girl, indeed.

She started to say something to Max, noticed his transfixed expression and grumbled beneath her breath. Such a typical male reaction. Then she shrugged. It would make a better picture. And she was photographing in color tonight.

"Hurry."

At Max's urgent whisper, Kate snapped the back of her camera closed and advanced the film. He moved aside.

"Great merciful heavens, she's going to fall out of that dress!" Kate was stunned, but not so stunned that she didn't get the camera to her eye, pronto.

"One can only hope" was Max's murmured comment.

Kate paused long enough to glare at him.

"I'm speaking professionally," he explained

"I'm sure you are."

The tone in her voice registered. "Have I mentioned how very lovely you look this evening?"

"No."

"You do. Very lovely."

Kate said nothing.

Max cleared his throat. "In fact, any man of taste would prefer your more elegant beauty to Fiona's rather blatant charms."

"That, of course, is why she makes her living in front of the camera, while I make mine behind it." Kate returned to photographing just as Damian leaned down and whispered in Fiona's ear.

It looked great.

With a giggle, Fiona straightened and hitched her bodice up, then kissed Damian on the cheek—presumably in thanks, but that wasn't the way Glen would interpret it.

It wasn't going to get any better than this. "Let's get out of here," Kate said. "There's an overnight courier service near the airport."

"Right." Immediately, Max took her hand and plowed through the crowd, Kate trotting behind him out the door and down the front steps.

Max spoke to the valet, and Kate fidgeted with impatience as they waited for his car.

"So, you finally got your picture," Max said after tipping the valet.

"Not exactly."

He shot her a questioning look.

"Fiona and Damian were at a public reception."

"So?"

As he drove away from the curb, Kate explained, "The pictures will look worse than they are."

"Glen's pictures always look worse than they are."

"But there were too many witnesses here for this to be conclusive proof that Fiona and Damian are having an affair. And *that's* what I've got to get."

"Look at this!" Max greeted Kate by waving a copy of *World Eye* in her face. It was the morning after Glen would have received her film and Kate was sitting in the hotel lobby hoping to catch Fiona as she left for the movie location. A long black limousine waited outside.

"Oh, good," Kate said when she saw the banner headline. "It's a special issue." Glen wasn't taking any chances. "He must have worked twenty hours straight to get this out so soon."

"Is it my imagination, or are certain...aspects of Fiona's anatomy digitally enhanced?"

"Probably."

Max made a mock sound of disapproval. "Shameless, utterly shameless."

"So is Fiona," Kate said, eyeing her pictures of Fiona splashed all over the front of *World Eye*. "I'm glad Glen sprang for colored ink even though my percentage will be less."

"Is that how he pays photographers?" Max asked. "A percentage of the sales?"

Kate nodded, curious that Max didn't already know this. "Only on the really big pictures—and I've just had a few of those. Otherwise, he couldn't afford to compete against the larger tabloids."

"Ah. I had wondered." Max flipped through the paper. "'Romance Between Co-stars Sizzles In Houston Heat'. Look." He pointed to a black-and-white photograph on one of the inside pages. "There's a picture of Fiona's husband."

"One of mine," Kate acknowledged. "I shot that picture of Winthrop shortly after they were engaged."

Glen had sprinkled in some of Kate's Italian pictures, as well.

"Do you think your brother will see these?"

Kate shook her head. "Not unless I send it to him."

Max started to comment, then stopped. "Damn."

"What?"

He nodded toward the lobby entrance. "We've got company."

A phalanx of news media disgorged from two vans.

"I guess they've seen this." Kate indicated the tabloid.

"Guess they have."

Kate silently watched as reporters and photographers rushed to the front desk. Hotel security tried to restrain them.

"Keep your eye on the limo," Kate instructed Max.

Sure enough, within moments, the car had moved away.

"Now," Kate informed Max, "you'll get a taste of celebrity chasing for real."

Walking slowly to avoid attracting attention, Kate led Max to the hotel kitchen delivery entrance where Fiona, wearing sunglasses and ineffectively concealing her hair under a hat, emerged from the service elevator.

"Here." Kate thrust her camera at Max. "You try to get her. Go!" She waved him off when he hesitated.

Max, like the pro he was, pursued her all the way to the car.

Kate could see Fiona's mouth open, but couldn't hear what she said.

Max jumped back as the limousine tires spun and squealed. Touching bottom as it exited the drive, the huge car quickly turned the corner.

Kate joined Max as he stared after Fiona's limousine. "What a filthy mouth she's got!"

Kate grinned. "Welcome to the world of the paparazzi."

The next time Kate saw Max, he was carrying his own camera equipment. He never told her exactly what Fiona had said to him, but he was obviously responding to the challenge.

Her impulsive gesture had rekindled Max's interest in photography. Kate was glad. Truly, she told herself.

Too bad they weren't the only ones following Fiona around.

"This is outrageous," Max complained. He and Kate had driven out to The Woodlands, but Kate didn't expect any usable shots of Fiona. "At least I now understand your partiality for trees and bushes."

News media were parked all over the lot and extra security kept any more unauthorized vehicles from turning off the road.

"One two-bit starlet two-times her husband, and dozens of reporters are sent to cover it," Max groused as he turned the car around. "Isn't anything more important going on in the world?"

Kate chuckled. As she suspected, Max would quickly lose interest in being a paparazzi. "Let's go back to the hotel."

"Why? Fiona is here." Max had pulled to the side of the road and was studying the perimeter of the parking lot. Kate guessed he was considering driving overland to a hiding place.

"Oh." She shrugged. "I just have a feeling."

He turned to her. "What kind of feeling?"

"Well, if Fiona were *my* wife and I wanted to remind her of that fact..."

"You'd pay her a little visit," Max finished, already putting the car in gear.

Two hours later, after a lunch of sandwiches in the hotel lobby, they were rewarded.

Kate grabbed for her camera. "There's the attentive husband."

A tall, silver-haired man entered the hotel lobby, a male assistant trailing in his wake.

"You *are* good," Max said with uncensored admiration, just as he put his camera to his eye.

His praise so rattled her, she let him get off the first shots.

*   *   *

The arrival of Fiona's husband—and Damian's wife and children—presented a united matrimonial front that Kate couldn't crack.

"So what's the word from Glen?" Max asked as soon as Kate hung up the telephone in her hotel room. "Are you staying?"

"Just until Cecelia Forbes's big charity gala this weekend." Kate was careful to keep her voice light and casual. "Then, it's back to Los Angeles for me." *Unless you ask me to stay.*

She turned away so Max wouldn't guess her feelings. She was becoming very adept at hiding her feelings from him, but she wished she didn't have to. Max was not an insensitive clod; he wouldn't want to hurt her. What they had together now was a friendship that Kate cherished and a physical attraction that made her blood sing. But now was not the time for them to commit to something deeper. If she tried, she'd lose Max as a friend as well as a lover.

So. Two more days. Two more days with Max. Kate knew he was restless. On their stakeouts, he now carried more equipment along than she did. He always reassured her that he just wanted a picture of Fiona for personal reasons and that he wouldn't intrude on Kate's territory.

She trusted him. And she loved him and it would hurt to let him go. Once she returned to Los Angeles, there would be a natural end to their relationship. Max had said no words of love, no words of commitment, and Kate didn't expect any. That's just the way he was and she'd rather have no promises than broken promises.

He stood, so she did, as well. "It would be a waste of time to chase Fiona with Winthrop shadowing her everywhere."

"I agree," Kate said, hoping that Max would suggest that they go to his home and forget Fiona for the next two days.

But he didn't. Frowning, he withdrew a notebook from his pocket and flipped through the pages. "Let's see . . . Friday is the twenty-third. The syndicate was supposed to send me releases to reprint some of those negatives for the retrospective. Tell you what, I want to check and see if the paperwork's arrived. Why don't I leave you to your own devices here, and meet you back in time to cover the gala?" He smiled as he closed the notebook and put it back in his pocket.

Kate forced an answering smile and it wasn't easy with disappointment flooding through her. *Get used to it*, she told herself. Max was already pulling away.

She'd expected it. Just not so soon.

Without Max's presence, Kate remembered why she'd spent weeks stalking Fiona. Not only would the Cecelia Forbes Charity Gala benefit performing arts in Houston, it would benefit Jonathan Brandon.

The entire cast of *Roman Vengeance* would be on hand, including representatives from the movie studio. Plenty of celebrities besides Fiona would be present and Kate could take enough candid photos to pay the rent for the next six months, maybe enough so she could afford to send her entire fee for a Fiona/Damian picture to Jonathan. The idea renewed her sense of purpose.

She spent the next day scoping out the Forbes mansion in River Oaks and looking for the best stakeout spots. There was the obligatory circular drive with wrought-iron entry gate. Parking valets and security would be stationed there, no doubt. Leaving her car down the block next to a catering van and two pickup trucks, Kate noted the companies' names, then walked the perimeter of the grounds. Landscaping crews positioned terracotta urns filled with flowers on the patio. Others raked the white gravel drive, removing minute bits of twigs and leaves.

And Kate found a flaw in an otherwise perfect yew hedge.

She was almost afraid she wouldn't, but near the far corner of the property, the hedge wasn't as dense. There was, in fact, a small gap. The gap was just big enough for Kate to slip through, although branches scratched and pulled at her clothes.

It was good enough.

Cecelia Forbes was famous for her rose garden and justifiably so, Kate saw when she stood inside the grounds. It wasn't easy to grow roses in this heat.

She studied the landscaping layout. People would tour the garden; it'd been mentioned in nearly every article about the upcoming gala. How could Fiona and Damian, separated for the past week, resist slipping away from their spouses for a moonlight stroll?

And when they did, Kate would record the occasion for posterity and *World Eye*.

On Friday morning, it rained.

By ten o'clock, Kate knew that she had to figure out a way to get inside the Forbes house. Even if it stopped raining, who would wander in the damp, mushy ground of the rose garden?

The newspaper society photographers would be invited to the party, but the paparazzi would be lining the circular drive of the River Oaks mansion, flashing photographs as luminaries ducked under umbrellas.

Kate wanted more than that. She wanted to be inside.

Figuring out a way to accomplish that helped keep her mind from dwelling on Max and wondering when she'd see him. She didn't know if it was possible to figure out a way for both of them to get inside, but she'd try.

Checking her notes from yesterday, she looked up the number of the caterer and called.

Kate's plan was to masquerade as one of the catering staff. She'd done it before—sometimes she'd even actually been hired as a temporary, but she doubted that would work this time.

It took some doing, but she wangled a two o'clock appointment to discuss a fictional cast party for *Roman Vengeance*. She slipped a black jacket over her T-shirt and slacks, added solid gold earrings and matching choker, clasped her hair at the back of her neck and gave a satisfied nod.

Kate invested in good quality black pieces of clothing. Black went everywhere and the quality allowed her to mix with anyone at any time. Although she wasn't on Cecelia's guest list, she'd attended enough Hollywood parties to realize that appearance was everything.

By four o'clock, Kate had learned that Fiesta Party Services used a traditional white shirt with black trousers or skirt for their uniforms.

Back in her hotel room, she was using an indelible marker to trace the Fiesta logo onto the pocket of the white blouse she'd just purchased, when there was a tap on her door.

"Ready for the big night?" Max asked after a too-brief kiss. He entered the room and smiled, his eyes not quite meeting hers.

"Just about." Kate studied him as she shut the door.

Something was wrong.

"Are your cameras out in the car?" she asked to break the silence before it had a chance to become uncomfortable.

"No." He shoved his hands into his pockets. "I booked a room here so I won't have to drive all the way back home tonight." Speaking quickly, he managed to meet her eyes and smile.

It was a fake smile. Kate knew them well. She pointed to the sofa by the window and sat in the chair at the desk. "What's wrong?" She laced her fingers together, indicating that she was ready to wait as long as necessary.

Max's expression changed. Mutely pacing a few steps before lowering himself onto the love seat, he exhaled heavily. "I was refused permission to reprint the bombing pictures."

"Refused?" Kate was stunned. "Why?"

"The pictures are still considered 'too inflammatory'."

"Lovely choice of words."

He managed a small, but genuine smile. "*International Journal* won't touch the pictures without the releases."

"But don't they belong to you?"

"Technically. However, the press syndicate holds first reproduction rights—which they have yet to option."

"Did you explain to *International Journal*? Maybe they could get permission." But Kate knew Max would have tried everything.

He shook his head.

"Max, I'm sorry." Kate reached out and took his hand.

He tugged until she was forced to stand and join him on the tiny sofa. Draping an arm around her shoulders, he pulled her close. "At least no pictures you'll take will ever be considered 'too inflammatory'."

"Hey!"

He dropped a kiss onto her forehead. "You know what I mean. With Glen, the more outrageous, the better. Anything goes as long as he has a huge liability fund."

He made a fist. "Damn the torpedoes and full steam ahead!"

Kate didn't feel quite comfortable with his comments, but knew he was hurt and disappointed. "It's not quite like that," she protested mildly. "We do have a responsibility—"

"Oh, Kate, come on! I saw what Glen did with those pictures of Fiona. A little judicious shading here and a little adjusting there...no wonder Fiona's husband hopped the next plane into Houston."

"Fiona shouldn't be carrying on with her leading man."

"So who appointed you judge and jury?"

Her mouth tight, Kate stood. "I realize you're disappointed about your pictures and I happen to be an available target. But however distasteful you find this work, it's what I have to do right now."

"I'm sorry, Kate." Max was on his feet at once. "You're right." He gathered her into his arms and Kate's anger left her as soon as his lips met hers.

He meant the kiss as an apology, she suspected. But on her part, there was only the quick flare of passion. This instant kindling always startled her. She waited for familiarity to dampen the desire she felt, but it only enhanced it.

How would she be able to say goodbye?

Her response took on a desperate edge that Max must have sensed. Breaking the kiss with obvious reluctance, he murmured, "I'd intended to take you to dinner. Any more of this and we'll miss it."

"I wouldn't mind."

Max groaned. "Yes, you would. We've got to be sharp this evening."

"You're right." Kate reluctantly slid her arms down his shoulders.

"I'm looking forward to tonight. And when I catch Fiona, I'm going to send her the photograph, with my compliments." He looked supremely confident, as well he might. "I'll change and meet you back here in, what, an hour? Will that leave us enough time?"

Kate nodded. "Wear black."

On his way out the door, Max stopped and turned to her, brow raised. "Naturally."

Kate grinned.

"Max!" Kate stood aside as he entered. "You're wearing a tuxedo."

"What do you think? Does it still fit?" He turned around for her inspection.

Like a glove. "Yes, it looks fine." Really, really fine.

"What's with the maid uniform?" He indicated her white blouse and black skirt. "I thought you'd be wearing that little black number you wore to the gallery reception."

Kate sighed. "Max, we're not going to the party. They won't let us inside."

"Sure they will," he said as Kate shook her head.

"You don't understand. *If* we're lucky, the press photographers will be allowed to stand by the entrance before they're herded away. I'd planned to get the usual exiting-the-limo shots, then sneak back in and stake out the rose garden. But since it's been raining, I don't think anyone will walk outside."

As she talked, Max had wandered over to the small desk where she'd laid out a shirt identical to the one she wore. "What's this?"

"Cecelia is using Fiesta Party Services. I'll dress as one of the staff so I can slip inside the mansion. I fixed a shirt for you, too. I had to guess your size."

He peeked in the collar. "Good guess. But it never occurred to me that you'd do something like this." He gave her a rueful smile and reached into his breast pocket. "We're on the official attendance list."

"We are?" She stared at the engraved card uncomprehendingly. *Maxwell Hunter and Guest.* "I'm 'guest'?"

He nodded. "You said you were on Fiona's no-admittance list."

"It was clever of you to remember." Kate heard the leaden quality of her voice, but was helpless to do anything about it.

She'd thought *she* was the one being clever. In her entire association with Max, she'd never been clever. Tonight, she'd wanted to impress him.

Returning the invitation to him, she asked, "How did you manage to get invited?" *That was stupid, Kate. He is Maxwell Hunter after all.*

He cleared his throat. "I imagine that after my generous contribution to the Houston arts, my name appeared on a list of easy touches."

"How much did this one cost?" She was being ungracious, but couldn't stop herself.

"Don't worry about it." He went to her closet and found the black dress—not difficult, since it was her only dress. "I have dinner reservations downstairs in the hotel restaurant in ten minutes. Will that be enough time for you to change?"

Kate stared at the dress and at the man who held it.

And she came to a decision.

Tonight was her last crack at Fiona. She wanted the picture, but she had to take it on her own.

Max's interest in Fiona was temporary, but for Kate this was more than a picture. It was a chance to right a wrong, to gain a second chance for her brother. She had to do this by herself.

And so she took the black dress and returned it to the closet. "I'll be glad to have dinner with you, but I want to finish this assignment my way."

"Why make it so hard for yourself?" Max was genuinely perplexed.

"Actually, mingling with the guests would get great party candids, but the kind of photographs that sell the best aren't of people standing around chattering."

"I know that, Kate," Max said with impatience. "But why sneak in when you can just walk in?"

"Because if it weren't for you, I wouldn't be able to *walk* in. Ever since we met, you've been smoothing the way."

"Of course I have. I wanted to make getting Fiona's picture easier for you."

She touched his arm to let him know she wasn't criticizing him. "Catching Fiona is important, but *how* I catch her is important, too. I've always been on a tight budget and so I do things differently than you do. I can't afford to buy opportunities the way you can, but that doesn't mean I don't get the job done."

He regarded her for a moment, then shrugged. "Okay. How about this? You go after Fiona your way and I'll go after her mine. We'll see who gets the best picture."

CHAPTER ELEVEN

"YOU from the agency?"

"Why else would I be dressed like this?" Kate wrinkled her nose and swept her hand down her prim outfit.

She'd deliberately approached the two harried men as they unloaded a white Fiesta Party Services van parked in the driveway next to the Forbes kitchen. She'd learned that busy people were not careful people. Busy people didn't have time to ask too many questions.

"Check in with Anna for your assignment," the man said as he hoisted a plastic fifty-pound bag of fresh shrimp onto a dolly.

That was easy enough, Kate thought, walking through the kitchen door.

In fact, it was a bit too easy. She'd simply parked her car down the block and had walked up the drive without being challenged by anyone. Where was the security? If she hadn't sought out the men, she might have been able to walk right inside the house.

The kitchen staff was just as busy.

"I said *spumoni*, not *baloney*!" bellowed an aproned man to an unfortunate underling. "What's the matter with you? You think people like these want lunch meat at a party?"

Kate scooted around the edges of the kitchen and stepped into a hallway. "Anna?" she asked of a man rushing by with a tray of glasses.

He pointed into the room he'd just left, where a woman dressed in black oversaw the placement of a temporary bar.

158

Kate approached her. "Anna?"

The woman turned.

"I was told to report to you for my assignment."

"From the agency?" Without waiting for an answer, the woman consulted a clipboard. "Are you Donna?"

Kate hesitated. "No."

The pencil moved down. "Lucia?"

"I'm Kate," she said, preparing to offer an explanation for the fact that her name wasn't on the list.

"Anna, we're short two bottles of scotch." The bartender leaned over the counter.

"How can you lose two bottles of booze just moving the bar in from the patio?"

The bartender spread his hands.

Anna flipped through the clipboard and scribbled a furious note. "Why is it always the scotch?" she asked Kate.

Knowing an answer wasn't called for, Kate shrugged.

Anna touched her arm. "Look, until I tell you otherwise, you're on dirty-dish detail. Sorry, but I don't have time to argue with you now," she said as she turned away.

Kate had no intention of arguing.

This was great. It was by far the easiest party she'd ever crashed. And Max had thought she'd have trouble. Now *he* would have to mingle with the guests while she had free run of the house.

Kate walked into the foyer, her gaze immediately caught by the curving staircase with the landing overlooking the front door.

What a great spot. She wouldn't even have to stand outside with the paparazzi; she'd be able to catch celebrities as they entered. Glen might not like tame photos such as those, but Kate knew other publications that did.

It was going to be a profitable night, she thought, walking right out the front door to retrieve the bag containing her camera. She'd hidden it, assuming that all workers would be searched, and she wanted to be accepted inside before drawing attention to her camera.

A search was standard operating procedure for Los Angeles gatherings with well-heeled luminaries. And here in Houston, her purse had been examined when she attended the art reception. But once the security guard had verified that her camera was really a camera and not concealing a weapon, she'd been allowed to bring it inside. She'd planned for a similar scenario here.

Now, she was wandering in and out of the house and no one had asked for any identification. Of course, the rain had contributed to the lax security, obviously causing a change in the party setup. Cecelia must have held out as long as possible before deciding to play it safe.

And Anna was harried. Apparently, Fiesta had hired a number of workers from a temporary agency, but that should be no excuse.

Kate actually considered mentioning something to a security guard—if one had been in sight.

Shrugging, she slipped up the stairs and sat on the curved landing, partially hidden by a wall. She'd shoot pictures through the banister supports.

From her vantage spot, Kate overlooked the entry and could see directly into the dining area, half of a living area and the edge of the bar. Directly below her was a powder room and tucked into the curve of the stairway was a grand piano.

Kate continued up the stairs. The window at the end of the hallway overlooked the rose garden and to the right was the back staircase.

Perfect.

*   *   *

Where was Max?

Had he decided not to come at all? Kate couldn't have missed him; she'd been watching from the landing since the first guests had arrived.

Was he outside with the local news media?

Had he been in an accident on the treacherous Houston freeways?

For that matter, Fiona hadn't arrived, either. Uneasily, Kate wondered if the two events were connected. Surely Fiona was putting in an appearance tonight. Or had Max discovered that she wasn't? It would be just like him, Kate grumbled to herself.

The party was well under way by the time Fiona finally arrived on the arm of her husband.

This was a subdued Fiona, playing the grande dame. Her dress was short and black, but conservative for Fiona. Her hair glowed with flames of its own. There would never be anything conservative about Fiona's hair.

Winthrop was himself a tall, formidable man with a full head of silver hair. Fiona clung to him like a limpet, her famous bracelet glittering in the light of the foyer's chandelier.

As Kate snapped photograph after photograph, Fiona tossed her head, revealing a sparkle at her earlobes. Kate zoomed in on Fiona's ears. Were these new diamonds to go with the bracelet? A peace offering? Was all forgiven? Glen would certainly think up a creative explanation.

Arriving directly after Fiona was Damian and a dark-haired woman, who held her head high. His wife.

The two couples made a great show of greeting each other as though they were all old friends. So that's the way they were going to play it, Kate thought, snapping her pictures. We'll see how long *that* lasts.

The two stars of *Roman Vengeance* caused a traffic jam in the foyer as guests drifted in from the other rooms to ogle them.

Grinning to herself, Kate caught several brocaded society matrons simpering as Damian flashed his famous smile.

On the whole, the entire party was a curious mix of old-guard wealth and the uninhibited Hollywood element. Raucous laughter echoed from the living area. The bar was well stocked, even without the missing bottles of scotch.

Kate lowered her camera. She had plenty of pictures of Fiona entering the party. Was she never leaving the foyer?

Fiona's husband and Damian's wife both held their spouses' arms in identical grips. Kate sighed. Maybe tonight wasn't to be her night after all. And it had seemed so promising. Surely if there were any justice in the world, she'd get *something* for Jonathan.

The piano music, rippling innocuously in the background, finally got on her nerves. Kate had just decided to leave her post, go down by the back stairs and actually collect the used glasses when Max arrived.

He stood at the entrance, momentarily blocked by the knot of people surrounding Fiona and her entourage.

How could anyone fail to notice him? To Kate's eyes, he was easily the most compelling man in the vicinity, actors included.

Impulsively, she brought her camera to her eye and photographed him. Max was handsome in a way that most men weren't. He'd lived life and it showed on his face.

And she could have arrived with him. Even now, Kate could be clinging to his arm the way Fiona clung to Winthrop's.

He bent to murmur in Cecelia's ear and she responded with a delighted smile, grasping both his hands in hers.

"Maxwell Hunter!" Clearly, Cecelia considered his presence a coup. She introduced him to a man standing next to her, and then to Fiona and company.

Kate watched Fiona carefully, but the redhead gave no sign that she recognized Max as the persistent photographer outside the hotel kitchen.

Max greeted everyone, then indicated the sleek black leather bag he'd slung over his shoulder.

The rat. Asking *permission*! That was cheating, to Kate's way of thinking. Also not very smart to alert the quarry. Didn't he realize that Fiona and Damian would be extra careful now?

Shaking her head, she watched as Cecelia and her husband willingly posed with the *Roman Vengeance* stars.

Posed photos. Glen wouldn't be interested. Hadn't Max learned anything from her?

Photographs taken, Max lowered his camera and the crowd milled around the stars again.

Several people briefly chatted with Max as he inched his way across the foyer. Occasionally, he scanned the crowd and with a thrill, Kate knew he was looking for her.

She remained motionless in the shadows as Max slowly turned, following the upper stair railing with his gaze until he found her. With a half smile, he inclined his head and strolled into the living room.

The pianist finished his set and left the keyboard. Without the music to cover the sound of her camera, Kate took the opportunity to stretch her legs and left her post to check out the window overlooking the rose garden.

Light spilled onto the tiled patio below her. The rain had stopped and it appeared that the French doors had been flung open. The glowing ends of cigarettes bobbed like fireflies. Good. People were moving outdoors. If only Fiona and Damian would.

"Having fun?" A familiar voice raised goose bumps along her arms.

Max had discovered the back staircase.

"Not yet, but I plan to," Kate answered, gesturing out the window.

"It's a great party," he said, handing her a glass filled with an orange liquid. "Very attentive staff."

"Ha-ha."

"Taste your drink," he urged.

"What is it?" Kate asked after she'd taken a sip.

"A bellini."

"Keeping with the Italian theme, of course." Beckoning for him to follow her, Kate returned to her spot on the stairs.

Max sat on the step above her, completely hidden from view. "It's too bad that Damian and Fiona have their spouses with them this evening."

Kate lifted a shoulder. "Those are the breaks." She finished her drink and set the glass carefully out of the way. "I'm not ready to write off the evening yet."

Within a few moments, the foyer thinned out. It was time to go downstairs and keep an eye on her quarry.

"Guess I'd better make myself useful," Kate said, adding, "I've been assigned dirty dishes."

Kate started to rise and felt Max's hand on her shoulder. "Sit with me awhile."

She had no willpower where he was concerned, Kate thought, sinking back onto the step. Fiona could wait.

"We haven't talked about what happens when you go back to Los Angeles."

Not now. Squeezing her eyes tight, Kate kept her back to him. "I'll turn in my pictures and hope Glen will pay me what they're worth."

"Kate, I—"

Keep talking. "Even if Fiona and Damian have ended their affair, Glen got wonderful mileage out of the gallery shots. Now he'll print the Italian pictures and keep this thing going for weeks." She heard a movement behind her and rushed on, "When he runs out of stuff, he'll start a rumor about somebody else and hope he's got the pictures to back it."

"I'm not talking about Glen," Max said, shifting until he was sitting beside her. "I'm talking about us."

"There isn't an 'us'."

"Of course there is."

Kate opened her eyes on a sigh. She felt like a deflated balloon. If only he'd taken the hint. But Max was honorable and wouldn't just let her fly back to Los Angeles thinking he'd call her. He'd want a clean break. She wanted to tell him this scene wasn't necessary, that she understood and anticipated the outcome of their brief association.

He took her hand and she was forced to meet his eyes. The gray gaze was as warm as she'd ever seen it. His lips curved slightly reminding her of the times they'd been pressed against hers. Kate's heart turned over.

Why did she have to fall in love with him?

He was about to speak and Kate interrupted him. She couldn't bear an it-was-great-while-it-lasted speech.

"How about you?" she croaked and cleared her throat. "Are you going home to plant those vegetables, or will you go back to photojournalism?"

"It depends on you." He gave her a look she couldn't misinterpret.

She squeezed his hand convulsively. "Don't."

"I thought—"

"Max, right now you're angry at your publisher and you think you want to quit. That'll change."

He didn't respond immediately and Kate sensed that he was filling in all the words she hadn't said. "Give me credit for having given this some thought," he said deliberately. "I'm tired. I'm tired of the constant travel. I'm tired of recording people's private agonies and I'm really tired of risking my life. It used to be exciting. It's not anymore."

He sounded sincere, but that was because he *was* sincere—right now.

"And censorship is an issue I want to pursue. I've been talking to reporters I used to work with and the stories aren't getting grittier—they're getting more homogenized." The noise of the party increased and he raised his voice. "I want to see news reported, not edited. So I—"

But Kate never found out what he was going to say. The rumble of noise turned into shouting and screaming. A tidal wave of people—guests, catering staff and kitchen help—flooded the foyer.

Kate grabbed her camera and started taking pictures without knowing what she was photographing.

A whistle tore through the noise. "Everybody shut up!"

Kate popped off a shot just before everyone froze. Three men, accessorizing the uniform of the catering company with ski masks, held guns on the group.

"Trick or treat, ladies and gents. We're going to pass the bag. Take off the jewelry and get out the cash. Everybody cooperates and nobody gets hurt."

Murmuring rumbled again and Kate took two more pictures before a hand tightened about her upper arm. Startled, she looked into Max's blazingly angry face.

With a jerk of his head, he indicated that she should move up the stairs.

And pass up this opportunity to photograph a society robbery? The pictures would be priceless. Kate violently shook her head.

The next thing she knew, she was being dragged bodily up the stairs, a hand clapped over her mouth. How dare he?

"Quiet!" Max breathed next to her ear.

Kate gestured frantically, but he ignored her until they were next to the window at the end of the hall.

He reached up and unlocked it, then slid open the window and removed the screen.

Kate pointed to the back staircase. Max grabbed her wrist and hauled her next to him, his voice barely audible. "I'm climbing down and I expect you right after me."

Kate glared at him and he tightened his grip until she gave him a tight nod.

He was insane.

He was going to break his leg.

But he didn't. His eyes never leaving her, Max buttoned his jacket over his camera and climbed out the window. After making sure she was watching him, he tested his weight on the patio cover, then crawled to the edge and lowered himself to the ground.

Before she could think about what she was doing, Kate had imitated his movements and found herself caught in a strong pair of arms. "I didn't know if they had someone guarding the back staircase," he explained, still whispering. "This way we can call the police."

Max held her close for an instant and Kate felt the pounding of his heart. He'd been frightened for her.

Pulling her toward the open French doors, they crouched in the shrubbery, concealed by the flower-filled terracotta urns. Looking past the bar, Kate could see into the foyer.

"Go ahead and try some shots," Max suggested. "I'll see if I can find a security guard."

But Kate already had better shots than she'd get here. She wanted to catch the escape. "I'm going around to the front," she whispered.

"Kate..."

"The robbers are by the front door. They won't run back through the house. I bet they've got a car waiting right there."

"They have guns, Kate," Max said sternly.

"I know."

"Guns shoot bullets."

"I *know*."

But Max grabbed her arm. "It's not worth risking your life."

"They won't even know I'm there."

"Then I'm coming with you," he stated in a voice that told Kate she'd only waste time arguing.

So she didn't. "Through the rose garden. I'll lead."

With a glance behind them, they started for the shadowy edges the patio lights didn't reach.

At the sound of a woman's laughter, they froze.

"Someone must have been out here when the robbery started," Max murmured.

They could hear the voices approaching.

"We've got to warn them," Kate said and started forward. Once again, Max detained her.

When she looked at him questioningly, he nodded toward the rose garden. Even in the flickering light of the torches, Fiona's hair gleamed brightly.

"I don't believe it," Kate whispered. What wretched timing. While she'd been talking with Max, Fiona had been cavorting among the roses with Damian.

Kate was almost sick at the lost opportunity, but she aimed her camera, just in case. Max had moved a little to her left, his own camera held ready.

"Where is everybody?" she heard Fiona ask.

"Who cares?" Damian replied, pulling her close. "Just as long as they leave us alone."

Fiona turned and melted into his arms, and there, framed by a bower of roses, Kate got her picture.

CHAPTER TWELVE

"THE police will want to see these." Max held a negative strip up to the safelight.

"So will Glen," Kate said, glancing over her shoulder and giving a little sigh. Max had removed his dinner jacket and tie, and rolled up the sleeves of his shirt. He was the only person she knew who could look attractive in yellow light.

She turned back to the images forming on the photographic paper. She and Max were in the darkroom of a camera store in a strip shopping center near Kate's hotel. While she'd been in Houston, Kate had rented time in the store's darkroom and it had given her enormous satisfaction to inform Max that they didn't have to drive all the way back to his darkroom to develop the film tonight. At last she'd thought of something before he had.

"Wow." At Max's low whistle, Kate left her print in the bath and joined him next to the amber light. "Kate, you just might have a license plate here."

After capturing Fiona on film, Kate and Max had run to the front of the mansion in time to photograph a Mercedes peeling rubber down the drive.

"The car's probably stolen," Kate said and went back to the print, surprised that she'd managed to photograph anything recognizable at all, her hands had been shaking so badly.

Max came to stand beside her as she immersed her print in the fixer. "Congratulations," he said when he saw a clearly recognizable Fiona, and her famous bracelet, with Damian. "You got her." He put his arm around Kate and pulled her close, nuzzling the side of her neck.

Kate slipped her arm around his waist and they stood together, staring at the picture. She waited for a feeling of elation to overtake her.

Fiona had used her brother, then discarded him without a thought when Winthrop came along. Jonathan's whole life had been affected. Instead of marrying the girl back home and leasing the small farm nearby, Jonathan was alone and working as a hired hand.

Fiona deserved this.

Kate stared at the picture of the flamboyant actress entwined with a man who was not her husband and felt nothing but sadness. Shouldn't revenge be sweeter?

Perhaps the letdown was because her success meant her collaboration with Max was definitely over. She'd go back to Los Angeles and Max would go back to his wars.

Max made a small sound and shook his head.

"What?"

"I was thinking that this picture will probably affect more people than any of mine ever did."

"Don't be absurd."

"I told you. I'm never absurd." Kate looked up at him and he pointed to the developing tray. "Think of what'll happen when that picture hits the stands."

"Winthrop will realize what a two-timer he married," she said, imagining the confrontation scene between a hysterically remorseful Fiona—she was an actress after all—and the unforgiving Winthrop.

"Winthrop doesn't strike me as a naive man."

"Love does funny things to people." She should know.

"He's chairman of the board of the Xavier Group. You don't reach his position without a certain savviness."

"His savvy was taking a nap when he married Fiona."

Max smiled down at her. "I don't think Winthrop is blind to his wife's faults. He can ignore rumors, but he won't be able to ignore that."

"Good," Kate said, adding, "He needs to know what's going on."

"Along with the rest of the world?" Chuckling, Max released her and wandered over to the negative strips hanging to dry. "Don't delude yourself, Kate. You might think you're doing him a favor, but he won't thank you for dragging him into a highly publicized divorce. On the other hand, maybe that's what you had in mind. Free Fiona for your brother?"

"I did not!" Kate denied. "Fiona isn't good enough for Jonathan!" In truth, she'd concentrated so hard on just getting the picture, she hadn't considered what would happen after *World Eye* published it. "*I'm* not breaking up her marriage. She's the one who's fooling around."

"Whether or not you intended to, you will," Max told her as he held film up to the light. "Her husband's too powerful and too conservative. If he ignored this, he'd look like a fool."

Kate felt an unwilling pang for Winthrop. She remembered the stoicly pleasant expression on his face during the party and tried to tell herself he'd be better off without Fiona. But that wasn't Kate's business, was it?

Max selected two negative strips to examine. "Are you going to make prints for the police or let them have the negatives?"

They both knew she'd have to surrender the negatives of the robbery sooner or later. "Prints for now. Glen gets first crack at the negatives," Kate responded, her thoughts on her brother, Fiona and Winthrop.

"Hey, here's mine." Max made a disapproving sound. "Damian has wandering hands."

Kate had forgotten about Damian and the consequences for him. Well, his marriage was already shaky and Kate doubted it would survive even without this incident. Unbidden, the memory of Damian's wife, head high, staring down the guests in the foyer caused Kate an unwelcome pang.

Max's picture was even more lurid than Kate's—naturally. She'd been concentrating on Fiona too much, while Max had been conscious of the entire scene.

"Old Glen will be mighty relieved to see these. It ought to put *World Eye* back in the black."

"Don't worry about Glen," Kate said, choosing another of her negatives to put in the enlarger. "He may talk cheap, but look what happened when you persuaded him to part with some up-front money." She smiled as she remembered Max's creative spending.

Kate's attention was drawn to the enlarged negative. She hadn't realized it, but this picture was even better than the other one. At least as good as Max's, she noted with satisfaction.

Fiona was doomed. And Kate couldn't imagine Winthrop backing any more of his wife's movies after this. In fact, he'd probably pull the plug on *Roman Vengeance*, or do his best to see that it wasn't released.

Again Kate waited for a feeling of triumph. She'd expected to feel celebratory. This was her champagne moment. Maybe she'd feel happier when she actually saw the pictures in print.

She'd exposed the photographic paper and had slid it into the tray before she realized that Max hadn't said anything for a while. Thinking back, she realized he hadn't said anything since the comment about Glen and money.

Max's back was to her as he marked which negatives he wanted to print. "Max," she began thoughtfully, "is Glen trying to weasel out of paying you your expenses?"

"No," he answered without turning around.

There was something hidden in that "no". Kate crossed the room until she could see his face. "Max?"

He wouldn't meet her eyes. *Back in the black*, he'd said.

"Is Glen having money trouble?"

"Does that surprise you?" Max lowered the negatives.

"He's always griping about money and threatening to sell out, but he managed to scrape together enough for me to..." Kate trailed off as she remembered how Glen had refused to fund her trip to Italy and then abruptly changed his mind and bought her a ticket.

She stared at Max.

He went very still.

"*You*! You paid for everything, didn't you?"

Max appeared as though he wasn't going to answer, then shrugged. "I expect to recoup my investment."

"You lent Glen money." A stunned Kate considered the ramifications. *Max's* money had paid her rent. *Max's* money had bought the museum photos from her. *Max's* money was paying for her hotel room right this minute.

Max winced. "It's worse than that. I now own a half interest in *World Eye*." His expression was wary as he waited for her reaction.

If Fiona had tracked her down and burst into the room, Kate wouldn't have been more surprised. Her mouth opened and closed. "Why?" she managed to ask.

His jaw hardened. "From now on, *I'll* choose which pictures I publish."

At last everything made sense. The only way Max could guarantee all his pictures were published was if he published them himself. *From now on*. He clearly intended to resume photography.

And he should. As talented as he was now, Kate knew that with maturity, he'd achieve greatness. Unfortunately, she knew he wouldn't achieve it with the typical *World Eye* subject matter. Did he?

"So the great Maxwell Hunter owns half a tabloid." Kate put the slightest emphasis on "tabloid".

"The great Maxwell Hunter is against censorship," he said, studying his negatives. He selected one, marked it and put it into the enlarger.

"Then are you going to print your pictures of the bombing?"

He sighed. "I can't. But I *can* print others I take in the future. Human nature being what it is, though, they won't have quite the same effect yours will."

"But mine aren't *important* pictures." Kate hoped Max would realize she was also telling him that pictures he took for *World Eye* wouldn't be important in the grand scheme of things, either.

"Sure they are. There'll be aftershocks for weeks."

The print floating in the bath pulled her gaze. Evidence of Fiona's duplicity. A private moment about to be made very public.

"Just think of the possibilities, Kate," Max continued, warming to the subject. "The movie will be thrown in limbo if Winthrop withdraws his backing."

All those people will be out of work. Investors would lose money.

The enlarger light flashed on. "It'll be years, if ever, before Fiona gets another role."

Her entourage will be job hunting.

Max turned to glance at her. "When she figures out you took the picture, she'll probably try to contact you. Are you prepared for that?"

Or she might contact Jonathan. With a sinking feeling, Kate envisioned Jonathan flying to Los Angeles to comfort a distraught Fiona—and blaming Kate.

"And who knows?" Max carried the exposed photographic paper to the first tray. "If Winthrop is involved in a prolonged divorce, Xavier Group's stock might tumble a point or two."

"Surely not," Kate said faintly. For the first time in her career, she felt squeamish about printing her photographs. Did she really want to exercise such power over so many people's lives?

No. She looked over at Max and, as always, was surprised by the strength of her feelings for him. Love. She loved him. Unwillingly, she remembered her conversations—arguments—with Jonathan. If her brother had felt for his fiancée anything approaching what Kate felt for Max, Fiona couldn't have tempted him.

He'd been foolish with his money, yes, but for the first time, Kate considered the possibility that he'd used Fiona as an excuse to break off an unwanted engagement.

She stared at the print. What did *she* want? She wanted Fiona to suffer as Jonathan had suffered. Perhaps Fiona was suffering now. She obviously wasn't happy in her marriage. But that was her business, not Kate's.

What about the money she'd get for the photograph and her plans to send it to her brother? Well, her other Fiona pictures should provide a financial cushion. Couldn't she share some of that with Jonathan?

Hating herself, Kate started to tell Max that she'd changed her mind about selling the picture.

Max was obviously unaware of her inner turmoil. "And closer to home," he continued as he swished the print from one tray to the next, "those pictures are going to save *World Eye.*"

Kate felt sick to her stomach. "Why didn't you tell me you were Glen's partner before?"

Carefully setting the tongs on the counter, Max put a hand on each of her shoulders as if he thought she'd run away. "I've wanted you from the moment you landed on top of me back on Capri. You hit me hard—literally."

At the look in his eyes, Kate's heart thudded.

"I wasn't sure how you'd react if you knew I was your boss."

"Half boss."

Laughing softly, Max drew her to his chest. Kate could feel his heart beating and nestled closer, wishing she could stay that way forever, wishing she'd never met Fiona Ferguson.

But Max wasn't a forever man, and until she'd met him, Kate hadn't known she was a forever woman. He wanted her, but wanting wasn't loving. In a way, she was glad he didn't love her. It would make what she had to do easier. She swallowed and pushed herself out of his arms. "I'd better make the prints for the police."

"Kate..."

He'd never said her name in quite that way before. His expression was open and vulnerable. Tender. His mouth curved and his eyes sought hers.

Her heart picked up speed. *He's going to tell me he loves me.* But no. It wasn't possible for Max to love her in the same way she loved him.

"We've got to hurry if I'm going to race back to Los Angeles on the first flight out," she said, trying to forestall him.

"Kate." Max tried to turn her back around.

"Just let me finish with these prints—"

"Kate, I love you." Max gently turned her limp body to face him.

She'd dreamed of hearing those words. She'd dreaded hearing those words.

"I've loved you since the night we spied on Fiona and Damian."

"Which one?" Was that gargling sound her voice?

"The one when you kissed me."

"Oh, that one."

"Yes, that one." Max bent his head and Kate knew he wanted to kiss her now. Of course he would; he'd just told her he loved her. But one kiss, and he'd know that she loved him, too.

She clutched at his shirtfront and tried not to burst into tears. Her eyes burned and her throat knotted. No, there was no way she was getting out of this without disgracing herself by crying. She didn't cry pretty. When Kate cried, she bawled.

"Kate?" Uncertainty crept into his voice. "I thought...don't you love me?"

"Yeees!" she wailed. "But I don't want to!"

Sobs overcame her.

Max held her close and murmured, his breath warming her ear. "Why don't you want to love me?" he asked when she'd calmed.

"Because I don't want to get hurt!" Finally voicing her fear set off another round of sobbing.

"Kate," he whispered close to her ear, "I'll never hurt you."

"Y-yes you will. You'll get sick of tabloid photography and you'll take off again."

"No," he said without hesitation. "No more wars." He smiled down at her, his gray eyes warmed by the amber light. "Anyway, I'm ready to settle down."

Though quiet, his voice rang with the sincerity of a true believer. For a minute, long enough to get herself under control, she allowed herself to hope.

But how long had he lasted in the home he'd remodeled? Once the work was done, he'd flown to Los Angeles. If he couldn't last a month, how could he last a lifetime?

The answer was, he couldn't. Kate knew this, even if Max didn't. He was the preeminent photojournalist of his generation. She couldn't let him waste himself at *World Eye*.

She knew what she had to do and she'd do it, no matter what the cost. No matter how much it hurt. No matter if she regretted it for the rest of her life.

With a supreme effort, she gave Max a watery smile and grabbed for the roll of paper towels to mop up her face.

"Are you all right?"

"Yes. Sorry."

"Kate, I want you to—"

Kate stopped him by taking both his hands. "We'll talk later. We've got a lot of work ahead of us if I intend to catch the first flight back to Los Angeles. Why don't you call the airlines?" Her voice was light. No betraying quiver. She was a better actress than Fiona.

Giving her a searching look, which Kate countered by standing on tiptoe and kissing him on the cheek, Max left the darkroom.

Before she could change her mind, Kate mixed a witches' brew of chemicals in a plastic tub and began dunking her prints of Fiona.

Then she started on the negatives—both hers and Max's. She lost time separating Fiona's frames from the robbery photos, but those would be needed by the police.

Max opened the door before she was finished. "What are you doing?" He crossed the room in three strides, and grabbed her wrist. It hurt.

"I don't want to use the pictures of Fiona," Kate said quickly. Better to get the impending scene over as soon as possible.

Max stared from her to the mess in the tub. Stone-faced, he plucked the remaining negative strip from her fingers and released her wrist.

Clutching the strip, Max glanced toward the empty drying lines. "You destroyed my negatives." His voice was flat.

"Yes."

Max's face was terrible to behold. "You don't have the right to destroy *my* negatives."

Kate blinked. She'd thought she was prepared to meet his anger. She wasn't. "I know, but that's what I did. Or just the pictures of Fiona."

"Why?"

He'd never understand, but she'd tell him anyway. "I didn't want the pictures published. I didn't want the responsibility for wrecking so many lives."

Max propped himself against the counter and folded his arms across his chest. Kate wasn't fooled. He was livid.

"So you, without discussing it with me, just destroyed the negatives."

"I know how you feel about censorship and—"

"Censorship!" Max pounded the counter with his fist, jiggling the liquids in the trays. "That's just what you did. You censored me."

Kate knew.

"Not only that," Max raged, "unless I can salvage something, you probably just did yourself out of any money."

"I know." Kate screwed the lids back on the chemicals. "I also know that you won't be able to forgive me. In fact, I wouldn't be surprised if you hated me right now." The thought brought no feeling with it. Kate was numb. She'd feel plenty later, she knew. Right now, she'd use the numbness to get out of here and go home.

As a free-lance photographer, she was finished. She might be finished with any photographic career. *World Eye* would go belly-up. She'd never work again, not after Glen finished spreading the word about what she'd done.

Since Max had probably invested most of his savings in the tabloid, he'd have to return to photojournalism to earn money. Once again the world would have Maxwell Hunter's pictures.

So neat, so tidy and so utterly devastating.

Kate hoped the world appreciated her sacrifice.

And she hoped that one day, Max would understand what she'd done, and forgive her.

She finished cleaning up. Max sat on the counter, examining the negatives Kate hadn't destroyed.

"I'm leaving now," she said into the silence. "I'll understand if you never want to see me again." Right then, Kate felt a double loss—his friendship as well as his love.

At her words, Max's head jerked up.

"You're a brilliant photographer. I wish you well." She turned to leave, feeling nothing. Absolutely nothing. Her emotions must have short-circuited.

She actually took two steps before Max blocked the door. "Where are you going?"

"Home." *Before I fall apart.* "I'll let you deal with the police. And Glen."

"Coward."

"That's right." Kate bent her head. "Please, let me go."

"No."

She forced herself to look at him, expecting to find disgust and contempt.

She didn't expect to find Max smiling.

"Kate, you funny thing."

Anger had made him crazed.

"You don't want the responsibility for affecting Fiona's life, yet you calmly wreck yours, Glen's, the entire *World Eye* staff's and mine."

Kate had been focusing too closely again. Not once had it occurred to her that people besides herself, Max and Glen would be affected by the demise of *World Eye*.

How stupid. How incredibly stupid.

"Kate," Max said on a laugh and folded her in his arms.

"How can you laugh?" Her voice was muffled against his chest. "Don't you hate me?"

"I love you, I don't hate you. I'm furious and I'd like to wring your neck, but I still love you."

He still loved her? Kate flung her arms around him and held him tightly, knowing she didn't have the courage to sabotage their relationship a second time. "I don't know why you still love me, but I'm glad you do."

"All you wanted was justice for your brother," he explained. "I guessed that you hadn't considered what breaking up Fiona's marriage would mean. I wanted you to be aware of the consequences *before* those pictures were published." He gave her a rueful smile. "I didn't realize you'd immediately destroy everything—including *my* negatives. We'll have serious words about that later."

"Is there going to be a later?" Kate asked in a small voice.

"There will be if you marry me."

Kate started to tell him all the reasons why their marriage wouldn't work. She opened her mouth. "Okay."

"Okay as in yes?"

"Okay as in I must be crazy."

"Crazy in love, I hope," Max said as he captured her lips in a long kiss.

"Oh, Max," Kate moaned, when they finally parted. "I won't be able to stand it when you're off covering a war."

"Kate, my war days are over." He touched her cheek. "I'm going to be running *World Eye* with Glen."

Kate winced. "There isn't going to be a *World Eye*, is there?"

Max laced their fingers together. "Come here." He led her to the remaining negative strip. "First of all, we've got exclusive pictures of a society robbery. That'll overshadow Fiona's amorous misadventures. Sales will skyrocket and you'll have money to send Jonathan, if you choose."

"Really?"

"Trust me," Max said. "Although don't be surprised if he won't accept it. I wouldn't."

"Why not?"

"Pride," he said simply.

Kate had never considered that Jonathan wouldn't jump at getting his money back. Maybe she could offer him a loan.

"Also, and I haven't discussed this with Glen yet," Max warned, "I want to take *World Eye* back to its news roots. The robbery will be a natural transition. Instead of being known for sensationalistic trash, I want *World Eye* to have a reputation for printing news with an edge, even if it's controversial."

"I *knew* you couldn't give up photojournalism."

Max smiled down at her. "But I might have, if it hadn't been for you." He squeezed her shoulders. "Look." He pointed to a picture of Fiona and Damian standing together on the patio.

"When did you take that?" Kate asked.

"Right after you started running through the rose garden. They broke apart when they heard the noise. We'll publish this with the robbery photos. It'll send a little warning to Fiona."

Kate shook her head. Max still had a lot to learn about selling tabloids. "There's nothing scandalous about that picture."

"Not to anyone but us and Fiona and Damian."

"Then what good will it do?"

Max grinned. "*We* know when that picture was taken and *they'll* know when that picture was taken."

"So?"

"So don't you think Fiona will spend days squirming and wondering when we'll publish the pictures we took of her smooching with Damian?"

"I love it." Kate's mouth stretched in a slow smile. It was brilliant. It was the perfect revenge. A little message from Kate to Fiona. "And I love you."

She leaned toward him, but he stopped her. "Kate?"

"Hmm?"

"I love you, but don't you ever again—*ever*—destroy negatives of mine." Max's expression was pitiless and Kate humbly realized what a devastating betrayal her actions were.

"I promise," she vowed. "I might try to talk you out of publishing certain pictures, but I won't destroy any negatives."

"Thank you," he said, bending to kiss her.

Their lips barely touched before Kate jerked back. "What about your house? How will you run *World Eye* from there?"

He regarded her with exasperation. "That house is my retreat and I'll keep it for us, but I wouldn't be happy living there year round."

Kate still wasn't convinced. "But you once thought all that peace and quiet was what you wanted. What if you change your mind about *World Eye*?" Or me? she added silently.

Max must have read her thoughts. "I'll always love you. As for *World Eye*..." He shrugged. "Some day I might want to move on. You might want a change, too."

Then he grinned. "We'll just have to see what develops."

EPILOGUE

A *WORLD EYE* EXCLUSIVE!

Famed Pulitzer-prize-winning photographer Maxwell Hunter married former features-photographer-turned-portrait-artist Kate Brandon in a ceremony attended by their families and the world's most renowned photographers.

World Eye asked each attending photographer to take pictures and submit one for inclusion in a souvenir album for the happy couple, which we've shared with you on pages four and five.

Congratulations, Max and Kate!

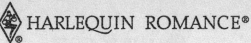

HARLEQUIN ROMANCE®

brings you

The written word has played an important role in all our romances in our Sealed With A Kiss series so far, and next month's RETURN TO SENDER by bestselling author Rebecca Winters (#3390) is no exception.

Unfortunately, what with Christmas and all, the letter in question has been delivered to the wrong house!

Sarah has never even heard of Mr. Jonah Sinclair, let alone knows why he is writing to tell her of his imminent arrival in Denver. By the time she realizes his letter had been delivered to the wrong house, it's too late, and a sexy stranger has turned up on her doorstep! And, unlike the letter, Sarah can hardly return Jonah to sender!

After the death of her husband, she had told herself that neither she nor her young son, Brody, needed a man in their lives. And yet Brody makes it clear what he really wants for Christmas is a dad. Her seems to think that Mr. Sinclair is perfect for the role. And even Sarah has to admit that there are some things Jonah is perfect at— kissing, for instance. Sarah can't help but feel that perhaps this Christmas, Santa has sent her exactly what she wanted....

"Winters weaves a magical spell that is unforgettable...."
—*Affaire de Coeur*

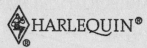

HARLEQUIN®

Don't miss these Harlequin favorites by some of our most distinguished authors!
And now you can receive a discount by ordering two or more titles!

HT#25593	WHAT MIGHT HAVE BEEN by Glenda Sanders	$2.99 U.S. ☐ /$3.50 CAN.	☐
HP#11713	AN UNSUITABLE WIFE by Lindsay Armstrong	$2.99 U.S. ☐ /$3.50 CAN.	☐
HR#03356	BACHELOR'S FAMILY by Jessica Steele	$2.99 U.S.☐ /$3.50 CAN.	☐
HS#70494	THE BIG SECRET by Janice Kaiser	$3.39	☐
HI#22196	CHILD'S PLAY by Bethany Campbell	$2.89	☐
HAR#16553	THE MARRYING TYPE by Judith Arnold	$3.50 U.S. ☐ /$3.99 CAN.	☐
HH#28844	THE TEMPTING OF JULIA by Maura Seger	$3.99 U.S ☐ /$4.50 CAN.	☐

(limited quantities available on certain titles)

AMOUNT	$
DEDUCT: 10% DISCOUNT FOR 2+ BOOKS	$
POSTAGE & HANDLING	$
($1.00 for one book, 50¢ for each additional)	
APPLICABLE TAXES*	$_____
<u>**TOTAL PAYABLE**</u>	$_____
(check or money order—please do not send cash)	

To order, complete this form and send it, along with a check or money order for the total above, payable to Harlequin Books, to: **In the U.S.:** 3010 Walden Avenue, P.O. Box 9047, Buffalo, NY 14269-9047; **In Canada:** P.O. Box 613, Fort Erie, Ontario, L2A 5X3.

Name: _____

Address:_____City: _____

State/Prov.: _____ Zip/Postal Code: _____

*New York residents remit applicable sales taxes.
Canadian residents remit applicable GST and provincial taxes.

HBACK-OD2

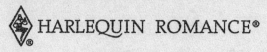

HARLEQUIN ROMANCE®

brings you

Romances that take the family to heart!

What could be better for Christmas than a warm and wonderful Yuletide romance with a man, a woman and an adorable little girl? Betty Neels's latest novel, A CHRISTMAS WISH (#3389), has all these things. Which is why it's our Family Ties book for December.

For Olivia Harding the offer of employment at an exclusive private school had come as something of a godsend. With little experience she hadn't expected to find a job so easily, let alone one that still brought her into contact with her former boss, the eminent Dutch surgeon Haso van der Eisler. Of course, his frequent visits to the school had more to do with his goddaughter Nel than her own limited attractions.

Nel was a lonely, fatherless girl, and that Haso should marry the child's glamorous mother seemed obvious to Olivia, but that didn't stop her wishing.... Would she find Haso or heartbreak under the mistletoe this Christmas?

"Betty Neels works her magic to bring us a touching love story."
                                        —*Romantic Times*

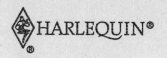

HARLEQUIN®

CHRISTMAS ROGUES

is giving you everything 🪝 you want on your Christmas list this year:

- ☑ -great romance stories
- ☑ -award-winning authors
- ☑ -a FREE gift promotion
- ☑ -an abundance of Christmas cheer

This November, not only can you join ANITA MILLS, PATRICIA POTTER and MIRANDA JARRETT for exciting, heartwarming Christmas stories about roguish men and the women who tame them—but you can also receive a FREE gold-tone necklace. (Details inside all copies of Christmas Rogues.)

CHRISTMAS ROGUES—romance reading at its best—only from HARLEQUIN BOOKS!

Available in November wherever Harlequin books are sold.

HARLEQUIN PRESENTS®

Harlequin brings you the best books, by the best authors!

LYNNE GRAHAM

Bestselling author of *Indecent Deception*

&

SANDRA MARTON

"Sandra Marton aims for her readers' hearts."
—*Romantic Times*

Coming next month:

THE UNFAITHFUL WIFE by Lynne Graham
Harlequin Presents #1779

Leah wanted a divorce...but Nik didn't! Why *would*
Nik Andreakis want to hang on to the wife he'd been
blackmailed into marrying? And why—after ignoring
Leah for five long years—was Nik suddenly making
passionate advances toward her?

HOSTAGE OF THE HAWK by Sandra Marton
Harlequin Presents #1780

Surely Joanna should despise Khalil? After all...the man
was holding her hostage! But Joanna had found heaven in
Khalil's embrace and now she wanted more...much more
from her "Hawk of the North"....

Harlequin Presents—the best has just gotten better!
Available in December, wherever Harlequin books are sold.

TAUTH-3